Do
Birds of Paradise
Believe
In Heaven?

Robert Shepyer

Do Birds of Paradise Believe in Heaven?

This is a work of fiction.

Copyrighted by Robert Shepyer ©2021

Library of Congress Control Number: 2021911022

All rights reserved. No part of this book may be reproduced, transmitted, or stored in an information retrieval system in any form or by any means, graphic, electronic, or mechanical without prior written permission from the author.

Printed in the United States of America

A 2 Z Press LLC

PO Box 582

Deleon Springs, FL 32130

bestlittleonlinebookstore.com

sizemore3630@aol.com

440-241-3126

ISBN: 978-1-945191-38-9

DEDICATION:

For Becca

Contents

Part Three – Nature as Media

"Only God creates. The rest of us just copy." – Michelangelo

Part One
Paradise as Adjective

1

About a Bird

When I look back upon my life as a Bird of Paradise, namely at my marriage to Sarah, I sometimes ask myself, was all the dancing it took to convince her to love me considered work?' All the books I read to display my impressive intellect, all the time it took to master my dance and honor our shared traditions. I did everything in my superb power to prove I wasn't just another bummy bird. All this had to be work, didn't it? I certainly ruffled a feather and paid a pretty berry pursuing her. Whenever this question weighs heavy on my mind, I turn to her and she looks at me with these certain eyes. It's the same look she gave me on that beautiful Papua, New Guinea sunset when we exchanged vows. That's when I tell myself I'd do it all over again, for eternity, because it's not work, it's heaven. No, not a day in paradise did I ever have to work.

***

I know what you're thinking...how does a bird read a book, let alone write one? How do birds marry or exchange vows? Well, first I learned English. I know it sounds unbelievable, but I was driven. I dreamed a book written by a bird would change the world.

For the longest time, I had no love for humans. They were our neighbors - living off the land on the forest's edges while we kept to ourselves in the canopies and mountain tops. We left them alone but they wouldn't show us the same courtesy. With long, sharpened arrows and traps placed upon our forest floor, they would take us and pluck out our beautiful feathers to adorn their heads and snouts as tributes. It wasn't until I met two that played with books and pens instead of bows and arrows that I found humans I actually admired.

One day, I swooped down upon an especially thick and pleasant-looking branch. The branch sang to me, telling me it was blessed with plenty of paradise for two birds to meet. When my feet touched down upon the tree, I took a deep breath of this courting ground and knew it was special. Sunny and tender, no Superb female could resist perching upon such holy wood. I figured that if I were to meet my soulmate here, our children's feathers would be more a superb cyan than even mine.

Already, I felt as though a beautiful pair of eyes was observing my every ruffle. So, I started putting on a show, hopping about in fanciful fashion, dancing on air, teasing my transformation to inject the air with intrigue. Part of my strategy has always been having a little bit of fun - you should make them laugh, smile, and coo. My only problem is sometimes I get a little bit carried away and forget where I am. There are so few predators around, Birds of Paradise don't sense danger even if it's right under our beaks.

I hopped onto a string concealed by a leaf and the string triggered a trap that clasped a net over me. In a frenzy, I tried to escape but there was no hole in the net large enough for me to fit. Then out of the corner of my eye, I saw her, hiding in a tree, watching my kidnapping in pure horror. A black stripe ran over her teary eyes. She watched as I was snatched up and taken from paradise. I could tell she would've chosen me had I not been so unlucky.

The humans that took me were not of the same family as the ones that typically hunted us for feathers. There were two of them - a male and a female, making different sounds than I had ever heard. They put me in a small wooden cage and took me to a little house right outside the forest.

When they stepped inside and set my cage down upon a table beside a warm and flickering candle, they opened the hatch of my cage to free me. Immediately, I shot out the opening and pecked at every wall looking for an escape. There was no way out though, the cabin itself was a very large and inescapable wooden cage. I must have tried to flee until the sun set when I became exhausted.

It was at this point the humans crowded around me, spouting all sorts of strange sounds but repeating "Abraham" over and over. I would later learn these sounds were called "words" and that "Abraham" was my name.

I had no idea what they were saying but their expressions seemed childlike, treating me like I was their toy. I was terribly frightened of them until the female reached over and put her finger upon my head and softly glid it down my back to my tail. There was no Earthly comparison to that feeling. Her finger was so gentle and calming. Loving human touch was a foreign form of paradise few birds ever know.

From then on, I was their pet and received their affection all the time, whether they were happy or sad. The love they shared with me wasn't the love a man has for a woman or the love man has for God - this was the love the soul has for nature, and to these humans, I was nature. What they didn't realize though, was they were nature too.

One day, I heard a rustling from a branch outside our window. I looked up and saw another bird. I'd recognize that black stripe across her eyes anywhere - it was the same female that witnessed my capture. She was filled with curiosity, trying to peek inside and get a load of a pet's life. The humans saw me staring at her and noticed a certain longing in my gaze.

The male then pointed at her then looked down at me and made the sound, "Sarah." I liked the sound of that word. I would do anything to trick them into saying it because the sound made me feel so whole. I would later come to learn that Sarah was the bird's name. The male gave her that name because Sarah was Abraham's wife in the Bible and because he saw in us the hope that everything could start again.

Part of being a pet is becoming domesticated. This is what began happening to me, a tragedy of the highest order. Removed from Papua's wilderness, where the invisible energies of paradise feed a bird's magic, my plumage faded into a sad and boring array of neutral colors.

Because I couldn't be free, I became consumed with the act of watching. Watching these humans and learning from them. I learned that this life was wrapped in a slew of mysteries that involved every living being upon the Earth. Human love being the greatest mystery of all. It was so complex, the range of emotions I saw them go through. They were angry one second, sad another but still happy together as if the whole world hinged upon the happiness of one.

The day the humans left me and never returned marked the beginning of my transformation. They just got up and left one day, shutting the door behind them as if they wanted me to stay inside forever. It was the most callous thing, taking me as their pet only to abandon me.

In time, I forgot their faces and how human touch and affection felt. It was funny though, even though I forgot how they loved me, I can't help but remember how they loved each other. I almost envied them and their human love, how it required them to express and embrace the totality of their humanity. As if to feel joy they needed sadness and to feel peace they needed anger. Through this, they come to know themselves more deeply than a bird ever does.

In my isolation, all there was to eat were the bugs that crawled in through the cabin's cracks. It was a diet unbecoming of a superb bird of any species - everything I took in only served to dull my senses and style. These damages could only be repaired by eating berries, paradise's super food to restore the glory of a bird's soul and colors.

These days were spent wasting time in lengths too long awake and too short asleep. All I was left with were these big tomes of paper that the humans left behind. Each one was scribbled with the juice of the blackest berries. One tome remained open on the table beside my tiny wooden cage. The book's name was Genesis - the first book I ever read, it taught me both Hebrew and English.

This is how I learned about paradise and why I started asking myself questions like 'Who am I?' and 'Was my Papua the garden depicted in this book?' Like this island, Eden was a perfect place, where fruit grew in abundance and animals lived in harmony. In Eden, nature and humanity became stronger together instead of apart. Then upon temptation, the humans were banished from the garden.

What could possibly tempt someone enough to leave paradise and perfect nature? After reading Genesis, I feel like I tasted a different kind of forbidden fruit - for now I see Birds of Paradise for what we are. I just pray I am not banished like Adam and Eve because once they left, Eden simply ceased to exist.

What makes Papua a garden of Eden? It's because the land, its creatures, and its crop set the right conditions for infinite growth without cost. The surplus of food and lack of predators makes survival the last worry on a bird's mind.

There are no monkeys to steal our fruit. No squirrels to horde our nuts. So, why not grow extravagant plumage and feathers? Why not devote so much time to learning and performing our dances?

It's as if we are coddled by Mother Nature herself. Birds of Paradise devote their lives to various, obscure dances and every dance holds a secret about the nature of love that spans across every species, from birds to humanity.

For me personally, as a Superb Bird of Paradise, what I do is coordinate dozens of feathers to create a mask that enchants a female. Human males do something similar, donning different masks and attitudes to portray a range of characters - whomever she needs. He can be strong one day, emotional the next, a boxer or a poet, whatever a man can dream.

It goes to show the miracle of nature, that something as organic as a bird's feathers can be created with the same intent as Shakespeare had writing his epics.

*****

I remember one thing my two humans would do while they were alive. They would write. They would stare at me, get inspired, and write down their observations. It was like their secret dance but with pen to paper rather than feet to Earth.

All alone, I would use all the strength and dexterity of my beak to pull open the hard covers of every book and examine each scribble inside.

I would stare at these scribbles for hours, developing my understanding of how they formed letters then how the letters formed words then how the words formed sentences and most importantly, how the sentences formed ideas.

After a very long, pained winter of reading, absorbing all the material present from the Bible to Bukowski to my humans' journal entries, love letters, and even their observations of me, I acquired an interest in becoming a writer myself.

"A certain juice seeps out of a bird's broken heart and this juice is so sweet it can teach the whole world how to love."

I believe that's what humans call poetry, both the writing and me. I was spellbound by literature. If I could write, I could show the entire world Birds of Paradise have hearts and minds. Then humans wouldn't dare defile paradise if they only read a book by a bird.

The only question remaining was what in heaven should a Bird of Paradise write about? I needn't look further than the question to find the answer, for what could a I know more about than paradise? This place where humans go after they leave this world as reward for their good deeds.

Birds of Paradise may be a little aloof, but we are all sweet, noble creatures. What would birds think of this human concept? An island in the sky where everything they ever wanted was available to them. Sounds like Papua, honestly.

Every Bird of Paradise knows heaven, but what about God? Does some great Creator take special care of us or are all our blessings merely coincidences?

My book would require me to ask as many birds these metaphysical questions as possible. I would answer things humans pondered for centuries - answers they would have if they were only part of paradise like me.

2

Journal Entry #56

The sword is mightier than the pen. You have no idea how much I wish I could trade a pen for something that could scare the wits back into the fools that did this to our world.

We all should've seen it coming. It was around the corner for far too long and the signs of it approaching closer everyday were right under our noses.

For fifty years, we were living in a seemingly impenetrable bubble. Since the advent of smart technology, many people in the West could follow their dreams without a moment of suffering from cradle to grave.

Now, after the collapse, humans are too far removed from nature to stand a chance of living off it.

To calm my shattered nerves and avoid this painful truth, I fondly reminisce on my life as a writer. Not many people ever read my books, but I still made a living - whether as an unpublished journalist or unproduced screenwriter.

Even into my forties, I kept my dreams well fed with fresh pursuits in film and literature. Every year I'd churn out a novel much to the financial dread of my wife. She loved and hated me for my writing. When I wrote love letters, it would remind her why she'd tolerate me writing novels.

I remember the moment we decided to flee Brisbane.

Birds began falling out of the sky. It was the first omen of the apocalypse to come. This just happened to all play out during Passover.

As a Jew, my atheist wife did me the courtesy of keeping my traditions alive in the home. When I recanted the Israelite's' journey over our Seder, I hammered in the point that when the Jews left Egypt, they didn't wait for the bread to rise. They listened to their intuition and escaped with their unleavened Matzah.

Listening to the wind, I started looking for safe havens for us to hide from the fall. No amount of money was too much for the sake of our permanent relocation. Something inside me spoke with deafening conviction, this chapter of my life was coming to an end.

I liquidated all my assets and made sure every dollar I ever saved would be at my disposal and found the one place where there was the least civilization to fall: Papua, New Guinea - an island off the coast of Australia.

My only knowledge of the island was that it was home to Melanesian tribal peoples and Birds of Paradise, rare species of birds that were considered nature's miracles for how diverse they became without sufficient scientific explanation.

Every species had such different feathers and individual dances, there seemed not to be any rational motivation for so much random adaptation. A place with such inherent magic and beauty was the best place for us to go.

I bought our tickets and arranged for the tribe to build us a cabin. It cost a great deal of money I was saving to produce a film but that didn't matter. We were already past the point of cinema ever being produced at all. The only pursuable dream I had left was writing.

When we finally found the nerve to tell our friends what we were intending to do, they thought we were bonkers and laughed at us for taking such drastic measures. They thought the black cloud hanging over Brisbane was only temporary and would blow over before raining on their parade, but it wouldn't.

Sooner or later, nowhere that the hand of civilized man had touched it was safe. The ride to the airport was quick and easy with empty streets leading us straight to the sky. When we boarded the vacant plane to Papua and sat next to each other holding hands, we made a promise that no matter what happened, whether this was all a big mistake or not, we would ride this decision out to the bitter end, for better or for worse.

Jacob Stahl

3

The Gap

The humans have been gone for about a week now. I've stopped hoping they would return and instead my mind is solely consumed on finding my next meal, hoping it loses it way and ends up in my cabin. There's not much to do but read, eat, sleep, or think here. I stare into the mirror and it reminds me of the river but unlike the water, when I peck into it, the mirror doesn't break. I looked at myself and saw I was grey, foul and frail. I prayed for an end to this prison sentence and never lost hope I would escape.

One day these delusions of freedom were made real and a giant black being came bursting through the door, snapping its locked latches.

This being looked like a human built out of pure darkness without having any sort of skin or flesh. It had no face, its surface shined, and its limbs were jagged, not smooth like a human's. Every time it moved; it made an unnatural sound.

The faceless one stood there in the doorway until finally making a move, raising its hand at me. Before I could experience what the faceless one's hand had in store for me, I was halfway through the door.

I would remember my captivity as a bad dream or

short spell of sickness. As for humans, I would always love them. Not because they fed me or pet me but because they would cry, laugh, kiss, and write books. I cross my heart and swear upon paradise, before I am dead, I shall be a writer too.

Like a bullet, I shot up the trees and breached the fog up to the mountaintops I missed so dearly.

As a grey, boring bird, no longer superb and barely paradise, neither females nor males paid me any mind. I was a fly on the wall, studying successful and failed dances, and it was like I saw my own kind for the very first time. I had so many questions.

A beautiful male Twelve Wired Bird of Paradise perched at the tip of a broken, brown branch. His black back and yellow underbelly painted the forest with a single fat blot of harmony between dark and light.

His felt-like plumage led down his back to twelve spindly wires sticking out his rear. Curious as to what his heart's purpose was, a female fluttered over to his branch and sat right behind him. A long grin ran across his beak as he briskly swiped his wires across her face.

"Bahahahaha," she chirped uncontrollably. "That tickles."

"You're so cute when you chuckle. Are those dimples?" he asked her.

"Mhmm," was all she was able to blurt out between laughs.

Her laughs subsided and whatever substance hadn't melted away was soon reduced to nothing as the two danced together, floating in the sky.

Once the dance had finished, the male Twelve Wired flew off to retire for the rest of the day. A long, perfect sun soak awaited.

I tracked him down and once he saw me on his tail, he stopped on a branch to glare at me, not knowing why such an ugly bird was bothering him.

"What do you want, foul manucode?" he growled at me.

"*Manucode?* I'll have you know I have just as much paradise as you or any bird on this island."

"*Right.* Why do you look so foul then? Did you fall out of a tree when you were young?"

"You should've seen me a few month ago, I was bluer than the sky."

"Are you finished wasting my precious time with your lies or are you going to tell me your coat was the color of the rainbow? What do you want?"

"I'm not finished. I haven't even started. I followed you to ask you a few questions."

"Why?"

"I'm curious."

"Birds shouldn't be curious. The moment you pry, you resist a mystery's magic and resisting magic is unforgivable."

"We'll see about that. First, I'd like to ask you about God. I take it you don't believe anyone created all this."

"As in the trees? The mountains? The birds and berries? All this? Everything? No."

"Where else would it come from?"

"Have you ever studied the way a berry grows out of a branch? Or a sapling out of the Earth? Or heck, even how a bird hatches out of an egg?"

"Yeah, so?"

"So, every bird has a mother except the very first Mother Bird of Paradise, and she, along with the plants, grew out of the Earth."

"A bird grew out of the Earth? Did someone plant a seed?" I laughed then continued, "If the Earth itself is our creator, what created the Earth?"

"I am one step away from kicking your butt off this branch. I try not to think about such questions because again, curiosity makes a bird resistant to mystery and mysteries are magic."

"I have one more question."

"You get one more."

"What's the best advice you could give a bird trying to find a dance partner?"

"Hmph..."

"Besides laughter being the key to someone's heart," I began to explain his advice for him.

For the first time in the history of this island, a male Twelve Wired Bird of Paradise, laughed like mad. His laughter ran like a current through each of his twelve wires.

"What's so funny?"

"Laughter is just a means to an end. Connection is what matters. When a bird dances, their dance must speak to a bird's soul. It has to make them feel special, unique, and one of a kind."

"So, you believe in a soul? A part of you that exists after your body has met its end."

"That's two questions, you only had one left...but no, I don't. There's no reason to carry on once we leave this place. If you can imagine something better, what exactly would it be?"

"A place without pain...not just pain from predators but the pain of rejection."

"Laugh the pain off. You can do that right here in paradise. Someday, you'll find a partner that looks past your boring feathers and she'll love you. Then you'll understand what I mean."

There wasn't much left to ask, I gleaned the inspiration I needed from him to write. The faceless one was gone by the time I returned to the cabin. It was mine once again to use as a writer's nest.

I needed ink and paper. I would gather up as many berries in my beak as I could before flying back to the cabin where I would regurgitate them into an ink well. I'd mash the berries with my beak until it became a pool of dark red juice.

Then, using the empty journals these humans left, I attempted to write, dipping my beak into ink and slashing each stroke of each letter onto the page.

I believe this was what humans would characterize as 'chicken-scratch.'

Entrance to paradise is a product of practice and every Bird of Paradise knows nothing short of excellence is acceptable so, I decided to practice until my beak-writing developed into a dance of its own, a languid, sweeping calligraphy as soothing to the eye as a Superb bird's cyan feathers.

Finally, I began what would be my first book with a little prose inspired by my encounter with the Twelve Wired:

A bird can hold the hardest crush. One that would make a human's seem so small. In her heart, that little perching princess, she sees us and imagines how our dances would sweep her off her feet. How our wires would caress and tickle her sweet, beautiful face

She needn't realize how beautiful she is, our eyes might as well be mirrors, we smile to tears at the sight of her. A true heart is all a bird ever owns.

Not bad for a first time. Then I wrote about God, heaven, and the soul:

Islands in the sky, suspended in the mist. The birds fly to the canopies where pain ceases to exist.

The Garden of Eden was inspired by heaven and Papua inspired by the Garden. The Earth itself was a writer, dreaming our home into creation.

This life, the birds, our love, all the growth around us, nothing but the dream of beautiful Mother Nature.

I think I have a knack for this.

***

Humans and male Birds of Paradise don't give their females enough credit. They think that just because one gender of the species is more flamboyant, the other is somehow less involved in what makes us so paradise.

Superb birds like me know the opposite is true. The ones being impressed are more interesting than those doing the impressing.

Ultimately, females decide the outcome of the species by choosing who will help them carry on their paradise. This way, they define what paradise even is. That's no easy task, deciding what we are and will become, it's a responsibility as grandiose as carrying heaven on your shoulders.

I had been writing in complete solitude for seven days. By the Sabbath, I had one page of book written.

If this book were to consist of two hundred pages, it would take two hundred weeks to complete and that's only if I was both lucky and talented, which I am not. It would shed years off my life.

The prospect seems scary but now that I've tasted how meaningful it is to finish a page. I can only imagine the feeling of finishing a novel.

I wrapped up a paragraph about women but now, if I wanted to continue, I would have to speak with one. Really talk to her - zero flirtation.

I flew out the cabin and wound up in a tree, scanning the scene for a beauty. Then, poking out the leaves were two long ribbons like heavenly antennas. I followed the ribbons down until they reached the head of a King of Saxony perched atop a branch.

This regal and stout fellow, sunk his head into his chin, letting those two long royal feathers on his head dance in the breeze.

As if the wind carried his presence through every

pocket of the forest, the hearts of numerous spotted females perked up, dreaming about how it would feel to dance with a king.

Catching me completely off guard, the fat little king took flight in a magnificent arc over to one of the female birds.

She jumped back as if star struck. Shaking the branch, the king began to wave each of his giant flag-like head feathers in the air. Every moment she became more unsure whether she would stay or flea.

Royals aren't too proud to beg though, bending his knees to bounce up and down, the king took a deep breath, filled his lungs then began singing the most insistent melody.

It sounded like rushing water charged with an electric hum. Not long after, the female couldn't help but edge…no, ooze closer to the king. She was won.

Not because she was impressed by his plumage but because she saw the paradise in his willingness to bend down on one knee and raise her above himself.

A king can have the entire world but for a female this special, he would have to show humility. They danced in a brief flurry, then parted ways. At which point, I took off in the direction the female flew.

After a cool pursuit, she stopped upon a branch and I found a perch beneath her to plead my case to chat.

"What do you want?"

"Forgive my curiosity but I have a few questions only a female can answer."

"You're not a King of Saxony. Why do you want to talk to me?"

"I'm writing a book about Birds of Paradise."

"What's a book?"

"Think of it as a collection of stories."

"That sounds like the Shade Song."

"Shade Song?"

"It's said the Shade Song was created by the first

Mother Bird. The females of every species of Bird of Paradise know a different verse of the Shade Song. We sing these to our young, but they never remember once they grow up."

"What's your Shade Song verse?"

"King of Saxony, so rich and royal, your song is sweet, your heart is mighty, and paradise bends beneath your wings. For every kingdom needs a king. To be his queen, keep him strong and never forget he's always wrong whenever he dares disagree with the whims of the Queens of Saxony."

"I love that."

"Whatever you do, don't repeat it. These verses are supposed to be secret. I'm only telling you because you're not my kind."

"I still have three questions. Do you believe in a paradise we go to after life? Do you believe in one being that created everything? Do you believe there's a part of you that goes on after life?"

"No. No. And Yes."

"So, you believe in an eternal soul?"

"Of course — what else determines if a bird is a king or pauper? They must be born for it. It's in a bird's soul."

"Then what becomes of the soul once this life ends?"

"They stay here in paradise. Maybe they become part of the breeze or the sunshine or the waves. Who needs to float up into the sky when this island is perfection?"

I went off to write in solitude for another week until my neck slowly hunched over and my beak dulled with every stroke. I felt a rush of inspiring and vital nectar pump out the heart of the Earth into every corner of the land. I wrote this passage after concentrating this holy and chaotic cluster of thoughts into finer poetry.

"The Earth hatched an egg of stone and moss, with rivers running down the round like cracks. Once the chick had breached,

the story of the Birds of Paradise was passed down to her from Mother Earth. The chick stepped out her sacred shell as a full-grown bird and gave birth to many children of many colors."

We define paradise with the Gap, the range of diversity between species. Differences in feathers, ribbons, flags, plumes, eyes, feet, masks, tails, wires, crests, and beaks broaden the gap's horizons.

The gap is what makes Birds of Paradise so special. Our diversity. When a Bird of Paradise becomes a writer, that too widens the gap just like a bird being born with strange, new feathers no one's ever seen.

As a writer, I too widen the gap, wearing my mind and heart like plumage across my chest. No one knows why our appearances and personalities are so diverse but perhaps humanity can understand what it feels like finding harmony despite being so different.

4

Journal Entry #1

Jacob is the writer, not me. Being a writer's wife, a little bit of talent rubs off on you. You read everything your husband writes and improve your ability.

Ever since the world was turned upside down, any bit of deviancy seemed so meaningless to me. Anything detached from love or compassion lost its place in life.

Politics felt as irrelevant as television scheduling conflicts. I blew the dust off my husband's Bibles and started reading the day after the birds started falling from the sky.

I can't confirm Noah sailed on an ark filled with two of every animal but what I do feel confidant saying is when humanity forgets their purpose, society crumbles from under them.

As a life-long atheist, I can't go so far as to believe in God but when I read the Bible, I believe in its heart. I believe the Book has wisdom has wisdom to teach, a way of guiding humanity out of perilous situations like these, which in their time were constant. Their stories can be our torch through the darkness.

That's why I listened to Jacob when he said it was time for us to leave before Brisbane started to implode and all the roads were congested by everyone's escape. We had to leave and go where there were no humans to interfere with the creation of a new civilization.

Uprooting our lives from Brisbane, Australia to Papua, New Guinea didn't upset me, only because a few months prior, Jacob and I watched a documentary on Birds of Paradise that completely enchanted me. They became my favorite animal after that.

These were the most beautiful creatures on Earth. I tagged along knowing his intentions were to make this some kind of apocalyptic writer's retreat, not caring whether I'd be satisfied sharing eternity with him or not.

What he didn't know was I would've moved only to an island to see Birds of Paradise even if the world wasn't ending.

So, now that we're here and have all this time on our hands, I decided to keep a journal of my own. My words won't be as poetic as my husband's, but I can promise I won't be as pompous.

Wendy Stahl

5

Finding Your Protector

The most amazing thing I have ever come to realize is how love can make a man so strong. It can enable him to demolish things twice his size. The more a woman loves a man, the more that man is capable of in the name of protecting her.

How does a woman find her protector? Not just her soulmate, but the heaven-sent soul made just for her.

She must recognize in him a sureness of body, soul, and mind - some holy ratio between wingspan and circumference of chest. These things can be inflated or changed to trick a woman but, in the end, even if the trick works, her protector will fight to the death for her and win so long as he has the proper guts.

These higher purposes act like a man's wings, for in the act of pursuing them, a man can soar.

If I want to find a bird like that, I know just who to study: The Black Sickle Bill.

Even with a long, curving beak to extract the hardest-to-reach insects and nuts. The Sickle Bill's enormous size is his signature. He finds a high branch sticking straight up toward the sky to perch upon. The cracking of his crowing sounds like rapid gunfire.

He's a gentleman disguised as a hustler. He strikes a

pose upon his broken branch and makes his body into a big black plank that joins the branch to make the sign of the cross, blazing through the forest fog like a monk's sigil.

A female with suspicious eyes and a cautious heart approaches him. He lifts up his wings to reveal his shielding plumage, expanding like the sides of a battle axe - he is a massive bird.

She accepts him as her shield and feels no pain - only tenderness and warmth. She sinks into the warmth and comfort of his soft and massive chest.

The Black Sickles spent what seemed to be just a blink of eternity together before they flew off and I made my way after the male to pick his brain.

"What was that all about?" I asked the Black Sickle Bill.

"When she was just a chick, her mother was captured by poachers. I held her long enough to absorb her pain into my feathers."

"Did you feel her pain?"

"I never feel any pain at all."

"I highly doubt that's possible."

"Perhaps it isn't but I'll never show you any sign I'm hurt."

"The only place you'd ever find without pain is heaven."

"I believe in such a place."

"You do? I didn't expect that. Most birds seem to think there's no need for it."

"Those birds know little of this forest then. There has been pain suffered between these trees so terrible it would shock them. I've helped many birds overcome such pains. It's my reason for being. We should all hope that someday, I won't be needed for such things. Heaven may be my only chance to retire."

Luckily for me, a female Black Sickle was softly humming from afar.

Once my little interview with the male was finished, I hid myself in a thick and leafy tree peering down upon her singing a shade song to her newborn.

"The sickle's crescent mirrored the moon as reflected in the waters. From those waters the Mother Bird drank, and the moon tasted sweet. So, we search for the love within the moon and water's meeting. Now that sweetness you will share, with a young and hopeful beauty, who sees in your feathers, a shelter truly."

The song bled of soothing harmony. I caught myself closing my eyes, breathing the poetry into every pore of my emotional core. The verses entered my blood stream and circulated through every inch of me, inspiring fresh links in new neural patterns.

I began to formulate a paragraph of prose in my mind:

A man of great strength and impenetrable will can defend his woman against winter's worst marauders. However, the man who saves his nuts high atop the mountain defends his woman from the winter.

Which offers a woman true security? In days of plague and famine, a barrel-chested giant can fall just as easily as an invalid.

It would seem then, a bird with wealth is preferable to a bird with strength. This theory required further investigation and if you're seeking a bird with wealth, look for extravagant ribbons waving in the wind.

For the Ribbon-tailed Astrabia, the forest's most debonair and dashing bird, paradise never takes a day off from being ravishing.

He puffs his chest just like Black Sickle Bill, but he doesn't need to. He does a little dance, but again, he doesn't need to. He's has the most bottomless pockets but has ribbons that stretch twice the length of his body to make him undeniable.

This gives a female every bit of fantasy she needs. She dreams of a permanent vacation, as if this life wasn't breezy enough. It would so happen, that this Ribbon Tailed Astrabia had the longest ribbons of any islander.

Thus, he wasn't met with a single female, but instead, he held audience with a lick of knockouts, all sitting atop a branch, watching the show. Below them, a few males, enviously crooning over the show with their envy wrinkling every feather.

The Ribbon Tail wasn't threatened one bit, he danced for every female sitting there, winking at the one he really wanted in the middle.

I suddenly saw wealth for the fleeting virtue it was. The Ribbon Tail was granted a dance with the female, but what protection did he really offer her?

He was much more concerned with his own display than her happiness. You can't be anyone's shield if you're consumed with vanity.

All that's meant to be consumed is whatever harm comes her way. You gotta be willing to give up your ribbons.

So, if you're looking for someone that makes you feel safe, choose the one without an ego. The Black Sickle Bill with the big shoulders will risk paradise to protect you while the Astrabia won't lift a ribbon.

Keep in mind, I'm not writing this book just for birds. I'm writing this book to show humans how to return to paradise and bring peace and tranquility to your mind, heart and spirit.

6

Journal Entry #61

As soon as we arrived in Papua, we met with the tribal leaders that accommodated us with the basic essentials we'd need to stay in the cabin they built on the outskirts of the jungle.

When we arrived there, we were surprised it wasn't some ragtag yurt they put together, but an actual cottage with all the little structural details a couple of spoiled Australians might require.

Upon arriving, we gave them the money, clothes, and food the tribe asked us for in exchange for their labor. Before leaving, they introduced us to Akira, who would be our guide through the jungle.

Akira was a Japanese photographer who arrived on the island right before we did. He would show us what we could eat to sustain ourselves. He would also show us how to find and capture Birds of Paradise.

We hiked high into the mountains one day and Akira climbed up a tree like a squirrel to set a trap on a branch that he considered perfect for a bird to dance on.

Within hours, we caught ourselves a Superb Bird of Paradise and we named him Abraham. When we brought Abraham home, we realized it was the missing piece to our harmony.

Wendy and I had our fair share of tiffs you see. It was a relationship built upon the worst of our compulsions but look how far it got us. We stayed together through an apocalypse, so perhaps the ends justified the means.

Once everything fell apart and we arrived in Papua, the very nature of our love changed seasons.

We worked to make the words that came out of our mouths filled with virtue and beauty, not filth. It was as if we knew that any ugliness we contributed to the world could force it deeper into this mess. Everyone was guilty of contributing to the world's end.

We gave Abraham all the love our hearts were overflowing with. We pet him, we kissed him, we fed him everything he could've liked. We played music for him and read to him like he was our baby.

Perhaps the greatest sign of our admiration for this beautiful little bird was that we wrote about him.

I devoted entry after entry to this bird, praising the details of his design.

Somewhere deep in our minds we felt a little guilty, taking him away from the life he was meant to live in the wild.

Compared to how he lived before, this captivity must've been rather bitter seeing as we gave Abraham a taste of civilized human interaction.

He would cower in corners whenever we argued but then once our frustrations peaked, we would only need to look at our bird to regain our senses. We were quite certain our Bird of Paradise was very curious as to how humans can be so hurtful to each other one moment then so loving the next. I wish I had the words to explain this complexity to him.

He inspired in us the most humanity we felt in a long time.

Jacob Stahl

7

Humans of Paradise

Why did those two humans ever come to Papua in the first place? What drove them here? They weren't on expedition. They were trying to escape.

You see, we are so remote here on this island, the various pains that end up bleeding all over the world, never wind up on our soil.

So, when civilization was compromised, these two geniuses came to my island and held me prisoner to entertain them during their quarantine.

Why did this happen to humanity? Did they do it to themselves? Mother Nature's revenge? As their own traditions would testify, humanity suffered because they forgot God. Many take that to mean man broke God's written law by loving the wrong person or eating the wrong meat but that's not quite it. Humanity forgot God when they stopped respecting each other and lost sight of the beauty in the world and the beauty in each other. They let the material world define their spiritual identities.

They never left the garden, they simply built so much upon it. The ground they were standing on was too far removed from God to feel His workings beneath their feet.

At the point in which their end was unavoidable,

humans had lost every notion of how to love each other. They thought expressing hatred and pride was the way to find love and companionship. Much of what humanity forgot about God was taken from them by the use of them using human media. Nature, on the other hand, has no media but itself.

To know the state of nature, all you have to do is tap into your own senses. Closing your eyes and letting the fresh air rush through your nostrils. This will inform you of the state of things.

For all the suffering I'm sure civilization's collapse dealt humanity, what is left of humanity will be closer to God's than ever.

Finally, humans will return to the garden, even if by a tremendous wallop. When this happens, we birds will welcome them to Papua with open arms.

What a Bird of Paradise can see in humanity's tragedy is how misguided they were trying to reach perfection, especially when it was their starting point.

The books of their traditions depict the beginning and the end as similar states of being. Yet, the middle, the unbearably long between, was filled with horror and mistreatment of their fellow man.

Maintaining the best of the beginning, keeping the garden alive and eternal, was the only way to reach the end at all. In this sense, reality's story should've never had a middle, nor a beginning or an end. It should've been one giant circle.

The story goes that man and woman were ejected out of paradise for disobeying God. Even in exile, humanity could've taken Eden with them and fashioned the land into paradise wherever rain fed soil.

These two humans arrived in Papua like Adam and Eve in search of relearning the old way. They learned a great deal simply by studying paradise.

To think a Superb bird like me, nature's most precious

mystery, is of "lesser instincts" to these humans. Now, from the ashes of civilization, a new blazing bird will arise. This new beacon of hope is humanity's openness to learn.

My book will reteach humans the old ways. It will be a guide to realigning their hearts and souls with nature.

The ways of the Birds of Paradise were once the human ways. Mankind once lived in harmony with the food they needed to survive, and it was provided to them in abundance, like ours. They once loved freely and beautifully like Adam and Eve loved each other. They lorded over the creatures then as they do now but back then, they never harmed a single one.

Mankind never found joy in any living being's suffering. They found joy in life's intrinsic beauty, which was everywhere around them, especially in their own hearts. These are the virtues of paradise, the secrets within every bird of this island. These were the commandments of Eden. Now that the civilized world has expelled humanity too, humanity must make new laws. I only ask them to remember how wonderful they once were.

8

Journal Entry # 2

As much as I love this new life with my feet upon the most fertile and spiritualized soil every morning, there are many things I miss about my old life. I miss television and social media. I miss 'likes,' 'comments,' 'follows,' and stalkers. I had so many of them all. I was a big deal on the internet back when it was the only recognized invisible connectivity between the world.

It was only when these foreign invaders appeared that all these dealings suddenly became completely arbitrary - but I miss the arbitrary, the shallow too. Everything is far too deep now. There's too much meaning to process.

Between my husband and I, how many hours of the day went to waste watching television? Especially in the last couple days before leaving. It took every bit of willpower to tear us away from our screens and make a real decision.

What we discovered here in the jungle was that, in the natural world, your body is the super-highway to knowledge. If you plug into nature, you will come to know your surroundings like they were as much a part of you as your skin.

The difference between nature and media is nature never reruns, it goes through cycles, yes, but it never repeats in the exact same way. No grasshopper takes the same bite out of the same leaf, no bee makes the same love to the same flower, and no Bird of Paradise dances the same dance twice.

It was once the case that every tree was wood for fire, every sacred indigenous land free to strip, every body of water was merely a place to dump the most toxic waste.

Humans had a much more difficult time seeing their favorite clothing brands fall out of style, or websites update formats, or celebrities be canceled than seeing the Earth toxify.

They warred over these things until culture and nature suffered in conjunction. Then, before culture could crumble, nature fell first.

My new life has made me see the light though. That God so loved humanity, he would test us to revive nature before letting come to a complete crashing finale. That God so loved humanity, He would sacrifice nature on our behalf, so we may regain our nobility by trying to revive it.

Wendy Stahl

9

Humanity's Saving Grace

I can't paint an accurate picture of humanity without mentioning their greatness in art and love. One begets the other, love is what stimulates art, so I will speak on latter.

It's not very paradise of me to envy humanity. There's so much build up to birdly love but little dancing to boast about.

Just as humans can learn from birds, so too can birds learn from humans. Being an observer to humans loving each other deeply together was the best part of my imprisonment.

I would do it all over again, just to see them close together one more time. Having birds learn to love each other like humans, meaning with commitment to a single partner, would be no easy task. It would take a bird denying their own instinct. To dance and dash is outdated programming in paradise.

One morning, after spending a sleepless night writing until my eyes were blackened and my beak turned brittle, I decided the time came to stop philosophizing about the meaning of love and act. I had to apply these new human virtues and break the rules of paradise under the weight of this new truth. I was ready to find love.

Convincing a female to love me the way humans love

might be a little too much to ask, but I have to try.

High up in the canopies, where the buzz of insects peak so persistently you have to consider it beautiful, there she was alone and eating, a starkly independent heart.

Sarah saw through this life's facade, that love was not just in individual birds - but present in all things around her. I joined her on a branch, and she turned to me with the courtesy not to run.

I stood there, fighting every impulse to raise my plumage as paradise rushed through my veins. I was stolid, my heart beating so fast it felt like the world was careening over. I refused to shape shift, our shapes were perfect as they were, oh so present in the now. I simply spoke, as a human might.

"Hello, Sarah," my chirps cracked.

Her chin shot to a curious angle as her eyes peered at me strangely. She was totally confused, for this was certainly against the rules.

"What did you call me?"

"Sarah. That is your name. My name is Abraham. Nice to meet you."

"A name? I have a name?"

"Yes. The way this piece of wood we're standing on is named a branch, your name is Sarah."

"I quite like my name. Sarah. I think I'll keep it. And you are Abraham?"

"Yes."

"What kind of bird are you, Abraham?"

"I am Superb like you," I said.

"Then what happened to your colors?"

"They turned grey when I learned to write."

"To write?"

"Like humans do."

"You emulate humans?"

"They're really not so bad once you get to know them."

"You're that bird they kidnapped and trapped in their nest, aren't you?"

"Yes. The humans saw you come to our window and named you Sarah."

"So, you were watching me?"

"Yes."

She flew away without needing to hear another word, making my heart sink into the quicksands of my chest. The birdly routine to deal with rejection is to carry yourself home and continue practicing your dance.

If I ever dance with Sarah, I will win her heart the human way. There was just something about that beautiful black stripe over her eyes and the zig-zagging brown strokes criss-crossing over her belly.

She sounded just as curious and willing to learn as I was - a heart like that, strong but open, is a bird I'd choose for a soulmate.

What a thing for a bird to say. Perhaps if all birds adopt the theory of a soul, dancing wouldn't be so brief or random. Perhaps the soul is the first ingredient to a relationship and marriage.

10

Journal Entry #70

My next book was going to be about a homeless person living in a tent in Los Angeles' Skid Row whose tent was in fact a portal to another dimension.

I wasn't sure exactly where it would lead but it would take each entrant to some place they needed to go.

My wife and I didn't have a portal, so we had to make our own passage to Papua. I'm not sure if I could write that book at this point.

The moment prior to destruction, the only thing that would've helped humanity evade this dilemma was a portal arriving out of nowhere.

Now that humanity's hit their iceberg, there is no escape - all portals are sealed shut and locked.

We've made our bed and now we must sleep in it. The key now is to slumber sweetly, regardless of what calamity occurs outside that sleep. For in a sleep inspired enough, we can dream our way out.

My sleep in Papua has been some of the best in my entire life. Like a baby being rocked by paradise's gentle breeze, Abraham coos at us until our eyelids fall heavy and we drift away.

What I dream in that sleep will be the subject of my

next book. So far, the dreams have all been as tranquil as they are bizarre because my mind is still adjusting to its freedom from invisible encumbrances like radiation and smog.

My first dream was of a boat, bobbing up and down in a calm sea. The sky was bursting with reds and purples, and a sun setting. I was alone on this boat when I heard a booming voice from the heavens telling me to look up. I raised my head and saw another boat, an enormous ark, cutting through the clouds like they were rip curls. The floating castle was filled with various peoples of every race and origin. Not one looked quite like the next. Then, at the wheel of the boat, was Abraham steering through the uncharted air.

If I wrote about birds, what would I even have to say? How much can someone possibly muse about a species of animal that can't even communicate?

Watching them all this time, they certainly aren't as complex as people. You stare into a Bird of Paradise's eyes just as patronizingly as you do a chicken. It's the feathers that snatch your heart up, make you hope the things can feel.

If I write a book here, it'll be a book humanity can use to save itself. Something we would need.

I'm not sure how suited I am to be the one preaching the answer but simply having survived up to this point should give me some credibility.

If only ghosts would read. The very first two hundred pages will be all about unlearning everything modernity crammed into our heads.

Once the slate has been cleaned of all that garbage and fakery, the feeling of inner peace you acquire will give you every bit of energy to learn new, beautiful systems.

Jacob Stahl

11

Darwin's Guide to Gardening

Charles Darwin always loved Birds of Paradise. We held the key to so many of nature's mysteries - our plumage, our dances, our paradise, all our strange.

Darwin's theories were integral to human understanding of Birds of Paradise. Learning about our origins gives me the keys to impart the knowledge that will drive our species into the future.

The same goes for humans, without the awareness of the cycle they're a part of, they can't move onto their next level. What that next level will be is one that is equally advantageous to humanity as it is to nature.

I'm beginning to think the Bible, specifically Genesis, was more a foreshadowing than a history. Humanity's next epoch, if they wish to have one at all, must be to assume their God-given responsibility to garden the Earth.

The plants and animals of this planet accept humanity as our rulers. If humans want nature's subservience, they have to keep this place tidy. Taming nature is difficult, but it is possible. Nature reciprocates human love, for man is made in the image of God and nature still owes its paradise to Him.

What exactly is the role of a gardener and how does man properly assume it? First, like every time the world has shifted on its spiritual axis, humans must look and listen within.

God speaks through intuition. Through crazed delusions one hears and masses mock. Once that little voice starts chirping and people come together, they cannot wait for the bread to rise. They must follow instruction and start a journey that requires them to leave the land of their fathers.

What makes this moment different is almost everywhere on Earth has exiled humanity. Almost every land is tainted, toxic and not fit for settling. Everywhere but the certain paradises of the Earth that have waited for humans all this time.

The humans expelled from the world of greed must rediscover a familial connection to the humans that have always been connected to nature.

The tribes of New Guinea, though often unkind to us Birds of Paradise, do not live to destroy nature. Humans of the civilized world must extend the olive branch and learn tribal traditions.

The best parts of old knowledge must be combined with the best parts of new knowledge to create paradise's gardening guide.

12

Journal Entry # 3

It had been weeks since we arrived on the island and escaped global catastrophe. All but us were caught in the fray.

We thought we were the last two civilized people alive, but we couldn't know for sure. The news, if it was still being reported out there, had no way of reaching us.

When the tribe introduced us to Akira, a Japanese gentleman with a history of photographing Birds of Paradise for Japanese nature magazines, we got a clue of what was happening in the world.

When Akira met us, he immediately started to cry. We couldn't understand him at first, but his phone did not require an internet connection to translate his Japanese into English. The sad truth was told to us by the most robotic voice, indifferent to all the pain it would describe.

As Japan was the first country hit by the catastrophe, Akira had watched everyone he knew perish while the rest of the world was not yet privy to the approaching storm.

Outside his windows, his country was on fire. When everyone Akira had loved was gone, he broke house arrest to embrace the onslaught of the elements in the hope of escaping Japan. The shock was overwhelming. Akira told us he would've sooner combust before he'd stop running.

By some act of God, he reached the docks and found a boat waiting for him. The further away at sea he sailed, the more life he would feel returning to his hurting organs. He sailed all the way to Papua with barely any food or water.

Now on the island, his life's purpose was no longer to capture images of the birds, but to distract himself from his own memory.

We asked him if he knew what happened to the world, what humanity's fate was, and he couldn't say.

He assumed the world's rich and famous hid underground while everybody else was forgotten in the turbulent sands of time. He was sure though, there were people like him that managed to escape with their lives. Where they were, he didn't know, but chances are, they were at sea.

One day, Akira stopped visiting us. The first few days without seeing him, we began to miss him terribly.

A week later, we were willing to venture into the deepest reaches of the unknown forest to find him.

Wendy Stahl

13

The Clay Pigeon

The forest was cooing me closer to get lost in its infinite green circuitry. In every fold hid beauty in excess. The forest seemed to know what I was up to, writing a book on behalf of its health, so it reciprocated my love with its own.

There were birds dancing everywhere, berries ripely bursting with juice and seed. As I flew through this messy heaven and closed my eyes to let my other senses guide me, I was taken to a ridge no Superb Bird of Paradise ever felt the need to cross.

Following the land's irreverent growth, lakes led to bends that fell into blinding green where a valley hidden in the fog and bogged down by holy tangles of flowers found me.

Finally appearing at the bottom of a pit of pure light, was a white clay statue of a bird covered in an overgrowth of moss. The moss served to decorate the statue, not to overpower it; acting like a Bird of Paradise costume covering the plain dove beneath.

When the breeze flowed through the dove's clay pores, it was as if the statue whistled in tearful reverie, filling the air with the odd reek of olives.

I hopped up the statue's body and made my way to its

beak, staring it straight in the eyes. I could sense somehow, looking into its clay pupils, it was responsive to my emotions.

Suddenly, the statue began to quake from under me with tremors as if its shell was molting. My presence had awakened its spirit and it was unhappy its sleep was being disturbed.

The statue's body began to crack, and the cracks ran all the way from the head to the tail until finally, it caved in on itself. The statue's face dislodged off the body and fell to the ground, shattering into a thousand dusty shambles.

I flew up to the hole where the face once rested and ventured inside its collapsed body.

The pungency of green olives fermenting for centuries smelled of a golden, sacred rot. Inside, I saw the dove's hidden treasure, a gift from God guarded by nature. It was a scroll written in ancient Hebrew.

I took the scroll in my beak and excavated it out of the statue. As I was ready to fly out, I saw her watching me, hiding on a branch. Sarah saw me looking back at her, but I made nothing of it. The scroll had to be taken back to my cabin and studied.

14

Journal Entry #78

It's been a week since we saw Akira and his absence has upset us worse than we could've ever imagined.

Our bird watches us like a warden, studying how depressed we've become. How am I supposed to write with my wife so upset?

We have decided we do not think this place is going to save us. Perhaps we are not worth saving. Papua is going to disappoint us like the rest of Earth did and we no longer feel we can escape the things to come.

I am so upset. I feel I was wrong; the Bible was wrong; my wife was wrong. Now, instead of lovely and welcoming, I find Nature to be against us and ultimately our enemy too - now, then, and always.

I realized the bird in the room is watching us, studying how evil we are. All of it, the Earth and its inhabitants deserved this fate. Every breath we take deserves to be the one we choke on. All my ranting and upset are not helping me or my wife.

Wendy has been crying in bed for a week now. After having to feed and wash her, I realized the only way to cheer her up was to tell her we were going to leave our cabin and look for Akira and we weren't going to return until we found him. This didn't make her happy, but it did get her out of bed.

I had a bad feeling about it all, but I didn't let that stop us. In case we never returned, I was going to make this a farewell of sorts.

So, if you don't find any entries dated after this one, consider this my goodbye. Wendy and I had beautiful lives together. The world for as long as we knew it certainly did not deserve this.

If it wasn't an accident, this fate was by the design of madmen. But I am not afraid, for goodness always wins. Evil men cannot overcome their own brutality. Sooner or later, the pain they create consumes them too.

It was the saddest moment in my life to think I wasn't a writer after all. I was a terror. I'm some kind of thing all writers ought to despise. I've been crying all day, just like Wendy, anticipating this moment's silence.

I consider the story of humanity a tragedy - ever since Genesis. Who did we think we were? We were gifted all this, an entire Earth full of food, water, shade, medicine, beauty, magic, and what did we do with these gifts but squander them? We really thought we could do better with skyscrapers, hamburgers, casinos, and every other impure thing.

The reality was humans that can't come close to reproducing any of God's creations. If there was a purpose to my writing and my life as a writer, it would be to live life to fullest. I now disavow every word I ever wrote in the name of living in the moment. My new purpose is this, with the very little time and words I have left, return to nature, forever.

Jacob Stahl

15

The Ashes of Paradise

When the faceless ones first arrived on the island, they washed ashore inside a massive black cube. It was a perfect shade of black and of a cubic shape that does not appear in nature.

No bird nor human knew exactly what to make of what they saw. The obsidian cube shined under paradise's smiling sun as it expelled ten giant faceless ones.

They entered the forest and walked around, like any human does, leaving ugly footprints and disturbing the scenery. I figured I was the first to encounter a faceless one because I hadn't heard a stirring from them again until a bit later.

Eventually though, the faceless ones encountered the tribes of Papua. The humans were frightened to death of the faceless ones the moment they saw them. They raised their bows without hesitating and shot arrows that didn't even leave a mark upon the obsidian metal skin of these faceless ones.

All the women grabbed their children and attempted to hide them in their shelters. The men shouted back to them, telling them hiding was no use. They told their wives and children to run into the forest and not look back.

With all the men standing to defend the land of their ancestors, the land they knew since they were children, the faceless ones simply raised their hands and from their palms, shot incinerating flames.

The entire village burned to ash and after, the faceless ones descended upon the forest and set it on fire.

The flames engulfed the forest's outer edge first, enveloping the trees in a glorious wall of fire and smoke that rose up to the island's highest peaks.

The birds above knew the birds below were in trouble and sang the alarm down a chain that descended lower and lower down the mountain ranges to the forest floors, begging the birds to leave.

The humans could not understand our urgent plea for all life to evacuate. They let their sorrow slow them down until they could not outrun the fire's barrage.

The birds flew in one direction - away. Their screams and cries sounded like a chorus as their homes were scorched to nothing.

Meanwhile, I was on my way back to my cabin with the scroll I retrieved from the hidden statue. I kept it gripped tightly in my claws as Sarah followed me a long way behind.

When I first saw all the birds flying through the tops of the trees, shouting at each other not to go back, my first instinct before anything else was to get to Sarah.

Without thinking, I turned around hoping to see which way she went but couldn't find any trace of her. Then the soft sobbing of a beautiful bird summoned me over to a branch below me where Sarah sat, crying over a fallen female Superb.

The bird was lifeless upon the aching forest floor. Sarah knew just as well as I did the danger that was coming but she chose to stay and mourn, even when the bird's mother had already fled.

For a moment, I recognized something unmistakable in Sarah, something rare and unique in birds - her humanity.

The very next moment, I dropped the scroll from my claws and grabbed her. I didn't ask for her permission because I knew I was her protector and to ask would have only wasted time.

"Where are you taking me?"

"I'm flying you to my cabin. You'll be safe there."

I flew so hard; I was afraid I'd break my wings before I reached safety. There was a certain strength I acquired as I carried her though, as if I could carry three times her weight and maintain this speed for as long as I needed.

Part of this strength came from the paradise rushing through my body; part of it from the thought of Sarah's love. But the strongest source of this strength was most definitely my desire to impress her.

My body and brain exerted every ounce of strength my soul could possibly imagine to deliver her home. When we finally reached my cabin, I set her gently down upon the windowsill.

"I have to go back for the scroll, stay here and wait for me," I said, totally out of breath.

"Promise me you'll come back."

"I promise I'll be back."

I shot up back into the forest's fray, maintaining the same speed I rescued Sarah with. By this time the forest had been bogged down by heavy smoke as the fires rolled through thousands of habitats.

I began coughing as I flew, my lungs filling with fumes that paradise could not have prepared them for. As natural as fire is, paradise was somehow protected from it for as long as I've lived there.

Not for a second did I think this was the end of paradise though. I knew paradise would go on. What I was unsure of was myself. I can't say I was positive I would survive my journey to retrieve the scroll. I wasn't even sure the scroll would be there waiting for me. I had to try though, something I couldn't explain was pushing me forward.

If I try to imagine what forces were pushing me, I think of my parents, or perhaps the Mother Bird herself, asking me to trust my heart for it would never fail me.

My heart told me the scroll would be there when I returned and as was destined, there it was. Char was snowing down from the canopies as fire painted the sky. The scroll was safe; though I wondered if perhaps it could not burn.

I grabbed it and flew back again to the cabin, faster this time than any flight of the night. I didn't want to keep Sarah waiting, I was worried she would need me again, all alone in my cabin. The fires would spare us that night, paradise had much different plans for us than to perish.

Part Two
Artist as Hero

16

The Call to Adventure

My only hope was that when I returned to my cabin, Sarah would be waiting for me.

When I finally arrived, scroll in tow, I looked around and didn't see her. I flew in through the window and figured she must've gone her own way. There was nothing I could do at this point but to hope she was safe.

One by one, I pecked the scroll's corners down to pin it into the cabin's table then sprawled it out to hop across the ancient Hebrew text.

The scroll was made of sewn together animal skins. I could feel spirit beneath my feet. The Hebrew letters lacked the vowels that were present in the Bible I had on hand, so it would prove to be a bit more difficult to decipher.

As I started reading from right to left, Sarah flew up to the cabin's window and perched upon the sill to watch me work.

"You really have a nice nest here."

"There you are. Where have you been? I was worried sick."

"I wanted to check if some friends of mine were safe. Is that alright with you?" she asked sarcastically.

"Sorry."

"What's it say?" she continued.

"I only just started."

"Do you need privacy?"

I let my heart take a second to decide whether she could witness.

"You can stay if you want."

I assumed she only wanted to watch, but she had a much more pervasive method of getting close to me. She flew into the cabin and joined me atop the scroll. Staring down at the letters, she curled her brow, perplexed.

"You're telling me these scratches make words?"

"Yes, this is Hebrew."

"Read it aloud."

"The forests were once submerged in ocean and the tides once met this land where the fog now meets the mountaintops that all my chicks dance and play upon today."

A chill ran through her feathers as she looked at me with eyes so big, the black stripe across them stretched into a perfect square.

"Who wrote this?"

"We can't know for sure, but I would guess it's the Mother Bird. Those chicks dancing atop the mountains must mean us Birds of Paradise."

"Keep reading."

"How could I not notice our island? It was a beautiful oasis poking out of the murky seas. No matter how hard the rain fell, paradise refused to fall victim to the flood. Swooping down, I broke off a branch from an olive tree and flew it back to the ark."

"I've never seen an olive tree anywhere on the island."

"That's not the point. Do you know what this means?"

"What?"

"The Mother Bird is talking about the great flood of Noah. She was the dove that led the ark to land."

"I don't know anything about a flood or a Noah, I'm

sorry."

"It's a story from the human Bible."

She stared at me with a wet and tender gleam in her eyes. I could see her heartbeat against the inside of her chest, it seemed soft to me, so it must've been making quite a thumping for her.

"What?"

"Nothing," she replied coyly.

I cleared my throat to keep reading, "It took many days and nights to return to the ark. I would chew upon the branch anytime I needed the strength to keep my wings up. There was nowhere to land. To rest was to drown, so I had every intention of reaching the ark without sleep. When I finally saw my friends, I nearly came to tears, I was so happy. I gave Noah the branch and he knew I found land, so we set sail for the promise of paradise. The world's first rainbow reaching from one end of the horizon to the other signaled smooth and safe sails ahead. The tides would lower, calm, and swoon from under us. The flood was over before we reached our destination and we arrived at a whole new land ten times the size of paradise. A land for all the humans and animals of Noah's voyage. When Noah and his crew set foot upon that land, I asked him for a favor. I asked that instead of joining him, to allow me to settle on paradise and start a kingdom for birds. Noah and God gave me their blessings. Then after settling in paradise, I hatched a bird of more beautiful plumage than the world had ever seen."

Sarah jumped in front of me, stopping me from reading.

"How on Earth did you find this scroll?"

"I don't know. It was an accident."

"I followed you there, what made you fly so far?"

"I was looking for something to inspire my writing, so I decided to look somewhere I hadn't been before."

"Unbelievable. Every other bird thinks exactly the

same but us. You and I are honestly different."

"I wasn't always this way. After I was kidnapped, everything changed."

"How?"

"I was kept here for months as a pet, that's why I think and look this way. As it turns out, a bird's paradise is just as much a consequence of their routine as their biology. When my routine changed, my paradise changed."

"Your paradise is a consequence of destiny. I've never been in the presence of more paradise than yours."

I blushed through my grey feathers.

"Thank you. If you don't mind, I need to finish reading."

"Oh. Forgive me."

Sarah side-stepped out of my way and I continued reading where I left off.

"When he was growing up and I would feed him in his nest, I'd sing my chick to sleep with a song that was as long as he was beautiful. I called it the Shade Song, as it always provided my chicks with shelter," I read aloud from the scroll, realizing the Mother Bird was writing about the very first Shade Song.

I looked at Sarah's stunned face and hopped over to the corner of the scroll where a small note was written and continued reading the Mother Bird's account, "You now know the origin of the Birds of Paradise. To learn our destiny, return to the place you found this scroll and sing the Shade Song in its entirety. You will then be sent on the adventure of a lifetime."

This wasn't just a story I was reading - these were instructions. The Mother Bird wanted me to collect all the verses of the Shade Song from the different species living in paradise and sing them to her.

If I did this, I would learn the destiny of Birds of Paradise and be set on an adventure. I suspect the adventure is part of the destiny, in which case we might be in trouble because the call to adventure is usually the only answer to approaching turmoil. I turned to Sarah, hoping she'd tell me our Shade Song verse.

"You know the Superb verse of the Shade Song, don't you?"

"Good luck finding a Superb female that will tell you our verse, it's against tradition to sing it to any male of the species," Sarah glared at me.

I squinted with quiet frustration, *"Fine. I get it. Tradition."*

I fluttered out the window, leaving Sarah alone in my cabin to see the place that formed her soulmate.

***

I went on my way to collect all the verses to the Shade Song. Flying above the forest, soaring gives me so much peace. Weightless, there are moments I can feel the breeze carry me, so I let my wings go limp.

This is heaven in a wink, a thing every human ought to know. Wrestling with my destiny, part of me wishes I could've just stayed a normal bird, Superb yes, but conventional in every other way.

Dancing, masking about, there was nothing in my past that could've prepared me for what I've been asked to do. I just wanted to write, you see.

Applying any ounce of energy to adventuring was something I avoided throughout my whole life. Especially upon choosing an artist's mission to write this book.

Artists can't be heroes, can they? Not in the traditional sense, at least. Writers have no expertise in sword play, all that pencil work makes for an all too stiff grip on a hilt.

The reason an artist cannot be a hero is simply because an artist's adventure is to create, not to go out into the world

61

and be anyone's savior.

Heroes and artists do share one characteristic, though. Usually, chosen ones are separated from their community to acquire an outsider's perspective and rule book. They see the faults their community is blind to and as it turns out, that way of seeing things is the only way to save the community.

Will sharing the knowledge I've acquired be the salvation of Birds of Paradise? Who knows how many thousands were lost in the fire and if things will ever return to normal? Perhaps they shouldn't go back to normal, things that refuse to change quickly perish.

I was given the gift of literacy because I will use it to create a revolution of the heart and mind that will change the Birds of Paradise forever.

I venture through the forests that were blackened and turned to ash. I shed no tears flying above them. I don't cry because to know nature is to see the growth inherent in everything. This forest is dead, but it was once glorious, bright, and full of life-giving breath.

What will come of all these broken and burned down land is calcium rich soil that will grow into strong and magnificent trees. When Birds of Paradise perish, the Earth is gifted many new colors to drink and paint with. You will see, once the saplings start to sprout and the trees rise out of the ash, the greens of the leaves and the reds of the berries will be hues so deep they will mesmerize any eyes that land upon them.

I only wish humans understood this about nature and could see a destroyed forest for more than just its present state. If they could see every previous and every future cycle of regrowth, nature would teach them that all things finished can start again.

The destruction created by the faceless ones would be forgotten in time. From the forest to the humans, that which paradise lost will be replaced.

When the faceless ones finally finished devastating paradise, they returned to the cube from which they first came, fitting inside as perfectly as seeds in a fruit.

Once shut, the cube tumbled back out into the ocean until disappearing through a wrinkle in the horizon.

As the wind kisses the bottom of my wings and my eyes crack open to be reacquainted with the majesty of this forest, I quietly accept my adventure. Who knows exactly where it will lead me or if it's even worth all the trouble?

I'll do as the humans do and live the story. I must find every species of Bird of Paradise and learn their Shade Songs so I can sing them to the Mother Bird's statue and learn the destiny of the Birds of Paradise.

Between every chapter of part two, I will share with you the new verses of the song I've learned.

17

The Goldie's Shade Song

The few of Goldie's Birds of Paradise in New Guinea are isolated from the rest. I had to break a real sweat flying east of the mainland, making my way into a neighboring island's forest where this yellow and red songbird called for every female on the island to come hither. It sounded like a chorus of birds but, when I reached their branch, I saw it was two males in duet, swapping vocals.

They lowered their heads to flash the bright red feathers that flanked either side. A female was swept up by the sound, she had a barring pattern on her underside. Both birds sang sweetly, but the bolder voice won the heart of a female.

Once they finished and she flew off, I figured the simplest way to get her to sing the Shade Song was to tease her and say there's no way she could sing better than a male Goldie. This was the Shade Song she then sang to me.

"The sun bursts with color and heat that stain a bird's feathersforever. It won't be long until these yellow birds turn red with passion. The chick we nurse and care for is the bird we gave up some great love for. So that chick must love its mother so much that it sings her praises its whole life."

18

Verses Without Chorus

It took forever but, by the end of the season, I collected every Shade Song verse from every species of Bird of Paradise but one.

There are thirty-nine different species of Birds of Paradise. I have thirty-eight verses of the Shade Song memorized. It's a rather long and strange piece of music and poetry.

The only verse I'm missing, the thirty-ninth, is the Superb Bird of Paradise's song, which is tightly locked in Sarah's heart.

I didn't know where to find her but knowing Sarah, she would be watching me somewhere. I figured the only way I could call her attention and draw her close was to be the romantic I've always espoused to be and dance for her.

I found a branch and started chirping in my love language. It had been a while, so my voice cracked a bit but that didn't stop her from appearing right on time.

"Let's see what you got," Sarah smirked.

I tilted my head back, pointed my beak up to the sky, spread my cape out, pushed it forward and let my once-blue, now black, crown-patch forward to spread across my grey cape.

Before I was kidnapped, I had the same cyan plumes that were standard to all Superbs. While dancing, we're supposed to look like a psychedelic, smiling mask.

Now, after my transformation, I looked more like a Rorschach test, black splotches on a white surface for the viewer to interpret into many possible and personal symbols.

I hopped around her and as she transfixed upon my body, I could see my plumage testing her. What did she see in me? What was the first thought that came to her head?

I never saw this expression on a female while being swept off her feet. Then again, this specific dance was never performed in Superb history because I was no longer Superb.

I kept bouncing about until coming right up to her and forcing her to look into the heart of the Rorschach. She accepted me as her sweetheart in that moment and we danced in a happy frenzy. I was surprised how naturally courtship came back to me.

When our dance was finished, the most marvelous thing in my life happened. Sarah stayed by my side. It was expected that birds leave each other once they finished dancing.

Meanwhile, in every Bird of Paradise's heart, this was the most heartbreaking moment of the routine. We were following the rules of nature when we left each other, this time though, we followed our hearts and decided to cuddled. We appeared different to each other in that moment. The facade was lifted. Everything was demystified.

"Why don't you go?" she asked me.

"There's nowhere else I'd rather be. Since the moment I first met you, you were always the sweetest and most beautiful bird."

She raised both her wings and spread them around me, holding me in a warm embrace.

"I knew you were my destiny for a very long time, Sarah."

"And I knew you were mine. I never had any doubt about it."

"I'd sooner break the laws of nature than leave you."

She rested her head on my shoulder and suddenly I felt at peace. I know why humans write now. I know why they suffer to put pen to paper.

This feeling needs to be shared as far and wide as possible. I could write about Sarah for the rest of my life. The beauty in nature is the same beauty I find in our connection.

Like the Bible, our love is a text full of meaning. Our love dictates how we live just as the Bible dictates the laws for human life. Our love is so deep it holds within it the source codes of nature, God and reality itself.

She pulled away from my shoulder and dropped her wings back to her side.

"You need my Shade Song, don't you?"

"Yes."

"I hope that's not the only reason you worked so hard to win me over."

"You told me you'd never give it to me. I know you won't."

"You're right."

"It's tradition. I understand."

"There is something I can do though."

"What?"

"Sing me the other verses and we will go to the Mother Bird's statue together. There, I will sing the song in its entirety."

"I found the scroll though. It's my destiny to sing it."

"We're each other's birds. We share everything, including a destiny."

There was a stretch of silence in which I relinquished my ego.

"Are you ready to hear the thirty-eight verses of the Shade Song?" I asked her.

"Yes."

I took in a deep breath and began to sing. It felt like it took forever to reach the last word of the last verse but as soon as I finished, she took off to meet the Mother Bird.

19

The Standardwing's Shade Song

There is little standard about this Bird of Paradise. Standards refer to the flanking white feathers that extend from their shoulders. The emerald green tufts of plumage on his chest only magnify this male's majesty.

I flew all the way westward to an island off the mainland to find these oddities of paradise. What was strangest about his radical display, was he shot off a branch through the forest until clearing the treetops then shot back down, fluttering his standards all the while.

There were many females watching, getting a vicarious hit of adrenaline. I asked one of the females that didn't attempt to engage the male for their Shade Song, and she sang this to me.

"White feathers to catch the wind and a lover's heart. Green paradise beneath white fluttering dove. Mother Bird and Father Forest come to life. Shooting high above like a star then back down to kiss the soil. No matter how high, its only with our dance partners we reach the peak."

20

Gathering Paradise

Sarah shot her way to the shambled Mother Bird statue in the most mysterious and distant corner of paradise. She had some kind of second nature memory, returning there as if she visited it numerous times following my discovery of the scroll.

Every graceful stroke of her wings left traces of magic dust in her wake, as if she carried all of paradise's secrets in her feathers.

If I am destined, so is she. What is a bird's destiny without their true love but a sunken ship with forgotten plans? Our destines are not the same but they cannot exist without each other.

When she arrived at the foggy valley and flew down to its lowest depths, she found a branch to sing upon so the broken statue could witness her.

From there, she sang and sang, all thirty-nine verses of the song. With each Shade Song verse, the species that verse belonged to perked up as if being directly summoned.

First, the males flew over from every corner of the island, some ancient bone in them was tickled and told them exactly where to go. All of them remembered their verses from chick-hood, feeling some motherly connection to Sarah as she sang.

By the closing verse, the females joined the males, stopping at the feet of the Mother Bird's broken statue. Once Sarah finished the entire song, completely out of breath, she looked around and saw herself surrounded.

Every Bird of Paradise in Papua was present, it was as if an island-wide meeting was called to order. She didn't know what to say or do, but the female birds all seemed perturbed to find a spotlight on her.

"How did you know my verse of the Shade Song?" one bird asked.

"And mine too?" another fumed.

"You're not supposed to know the King of Saxony's song, you're a Superb bird, not a queen!"

The females were enraged but, before the scene could descend into chaos, this odd chirping came from the broken dove statue, distracting the angry mob.

From out a hole in the statue hopped a porcelain-white dove, a being so pure, any color would've detracted from its paradise.

"Leave her alone. She is worthy of every verse of the song," the bird had the most kind and motherly cadence in her voice. The mere sound of it nurtured us all like a bottle of milk does a newborn human.

When the dove said this, no Bird of Paradise dared question her. It was as if her radiance demanded obedience. The dove hopped up the statue until reaching Sarah to stand beside her.

"Why, you're so beautiful," the dove said to Sarah then turned to me, "You're a very lucky bird."

"Thank you," Sarah and I dually replied.

"Don't you all recognize me, my chicks?"

All in unison, the males spoke in one massive boom that shook the leaves like a strong wind.

"Mama," we all said together, almost chanting it.

"Yes, it is me. It does my old heart well to see all my chicks together at once. You've grown up to look so different."

"We knew we would see you again someday, Mother Bird," I told her.

"Of course. After all, you summoned me."

"I did what the scroll asked me to do. I didn't know it would bring you here."

"You mean you don't know what you summoned me for? You're not aware of your own purpose?"

"I'm writing a book. That's my purpose."

"Hear that my chicks? Your brother is writing a book," she reiterated to the flock then turned back to me to ask, "Why?"

"To teach humanity a new way of being."

"That makes sense. I am only ever to be summoned if humanity is in trouble. Otherwise, I need my beauty sleep."

"Will you be helping me write my book then?"

"I'll be helping you with much more than that. First, I need the consensus of the Birds of Paradise on a certain matter."

"What?"

"My chicks, I know you've all been affected by this recent tragedy. Many of your brothers and sisters left you to join me in the spirit world.

For so long, we thought nothing could hurt us in paradise but that is not true. We need something, or someone to protect our paradise.

That's why I ask you all, would any of you object to sharing this island with the humans who have escaped the fallen world and are looking for a new land to call home?"

There was a roar of chatter and descent among the birds. Some were paradise enough to welcome any creature that wanted to call Papua home, others were familiar with humanity's destructive habits and did not want paradise turned into another wasteland.

"Humans and birds will never get along. The reason there was a fire in the first place was because of humanity's dealings. They would not share the land with us, they would steal it even if we welcomed them with open wings," one bird contested.

"Have any of you seen how humans live? They destroy nature everywhere they go. They are more comfortable in chaos than paradise," another surmised.

"I have seen how humans live. I love humanity," I finally spoke up.

"Then speak. Why would you share this land with them?" the Mother Bird asked me.

"Nature is their mother just as much as it is ours. They can come to respect it again if they are taught how."

"Respect it again? When have they ever respected it?" a contrarian bird asked me.

"If you read their stories, you will see, they are filled with plenty of paradise. Some humans simply forgot how to tap into it," I replied.

"So, what you're saying is the human race is not prepared to return to paradise. If that's the case, we cannot allow them to enter our home."

"I will prepare them," I assured them.

"How can we trust you?"

"Look how far I've taken us already. I have summoned the Mother Bird back to her chicks."

The Birds of Paradise couldn't help but see my point with the Mother Bird standing right there in the flesh.

"I have given the Birds of Paradise a purpose and a story all their own. An origin. A destiny…and that destiny is to save humanity, for if we do so, they will save us as well. In teaching them, they will teach us."

"Teach us what? Save us how?"

"Humanity will teach the Birds of Paradise how to love

only one bird for the rest of their lives."

A hush fell over the crowd. They stared at me with beady little eyes until finally, in one euphoric burst, every male on the island, bird or not, began laughing at me with thunderous bellows. I was afraid these birds would choke they cackled so hard, spitting everywhere.

"You've got to be kidding me."

"This bird must be out of his mind."

"Are you sure you're a Bird of Paradise?"

Defeated, I hung my head; then looked up at Sarah. Tears were forming in her eyes. Not just hers though, every female in the forest began tearing up at the proposition. Then, all together, every female pecked at a male and they closed their egotistical traps straight away.

"Shut your stupid beaks!" the females screamed into the idiotic ears of every male, "He's talking about the exact same things you've been telling us that you always wanted. Did you really think we'd stop believing you after all this time? Well, now our day has come. We won't be anybody's fools, not after today. Every female is going to put their foot down and make this their last stand. There's finally going to be some accountability around here. That's the one thing paradise is lacking. You male birds have it so easy. Where are you while we're raising your chicks. Well, you're going to start showing up because if you don't commit to one bird each, none of you morons will get our undivided attention ever again," Sarah delivered the speech of her life and no bird was fearless enough to contest it.

The males all gasped. Their fear was palpable - even I started to tremble before Sarah's undisputed power.

"So, what's it going to be? Are you with us or against us?"

All the males looked between themselves, searching for an answer. Who was going to put their neck on the line and agree first? The bird that spoke first could risk being verbally torn to shreds if everyone else wasn't on board with them. Finally, sensing their dismay and weakness, the Mother Bird stepped forward to comfort her chicks.

"There, there, boys. It won't be so bad."

A collective sigh blew the leaves up from the soil and all at once the males of paradise surrendered, "*Fiiiiine.*"

"So, it's settled, the Birds of Paradise agree to share the islands with the human refugees and in exchange for our teachings of the ways of nature, they will teach us the ways of monogamy," the Mother Bird clapped her wings and that was that.

She then turned to me and smiled.

"You will have to find a branch to carry on your long journey out to sea. You will not know where to find these humans but, if you follow your paradise, it will lead you to them. Once you find them, bring them back home."

"I will," I replied.

The Mother Bird nodded and like magic, she turned into a pile of dust right in front of every Bird of Paradise.

We were unsure if what we experienced was real or some collective dream, but either way, no one dared oppose their mother's wishes.

They all scattered and went on their merry ways. For the rest of the day, not a single bird danced or spoke to each other. Why? Because every male had far too much soul searching to do on who and how to love forever.

While the males did this, the females dreamed the day away, wondering who their last dance would be with.

21

The Magnificent's Shade Song

Laying low by the forest floor, I found a Magnificent Bird of Paradise, clearing its court of everything that would make it seem untidy in a female's magnificent eyes. These ravishing emerald oddballs are as green as the deepest lagoons.

These birds like their soil with a steep slope. They find a sapling sticking out of the ground and climb up the stem just to show females how light on their feet they are.

Gracefully, the sapling doesn't wilt an inch under the bird's weight. When the bird reaches the sapling's head, they stretch out their vibrant green plumage like a cape and hang their head to let the shine of the yellow halo on their heads bounce off the green cape's gloss. It's a spiritual experience, seeing such magnificence.

Once they danced their Magnificent dance and the female fled back up the trees, I asked her for her Shade Song, saying it would be a blessing.

"The eyes of paradise shine a deep green as they sing the song of the spirit. A halo above a bird's head must mean the spirit heard the song. Those from the shade now see the light, so magnificent and full of glory. A Bird of Paradise with feathers so green, climbs a sapling to preach the spirit's love of music.

22

In Search of Man

Facing the greatest challenge of my little life with absolutely no experiences to prepare me, I was ready to take flight in search of mankind. I had to choose a branch to greet humanity with. I chose the Malay Apple's. Sweet and mild, these apples always tranquilize me.

I figured by now, humans must've experienced a long duration of pain, shock, terror, trauma and paranoia so, they should be greeted with a symbol of calming reassurance.

With branch in beak, I stood atop a hill overlooking the ocean. Sarah was with me to wish me good luck and goodbye.

"I will be waiting for you right here."

"No matter what happens. I will always love you and only you."

"I love you too, Abraham…if you do not come back…I will have no one.…"

She started to softly weep and I nuzzled my head against hers as if her skull housed her aching, worried heart.

"Don't cry. The Birds of Paradise are not destined for anything short of a happy ending. In our hearts we both know this. We have to trust it."

"I do."

I kissed her on the cheek. "Goodbye, my love."

"Goodbye," she said as she kissed me one last time.

I ran up the hill and jumped off the edge to take flight over the ocean. Birds of Paradise are not built for such journeys, but I had no choice.

Mile after mile, there was only ocean beneath my belly. Whenever I got tired, I would chew upon the branch and suck in whatever liquid manna it would produce. Even the tiniest drop would fuel another half day of painful flight.

The constant pushing of the waves backward would push my spirit forward. Adversity only fueled my drive. I felt so strong and stubborn, I would've scared the other birds, even Sarah, with how savage I made myself.

The few times I saw land, they would appear as small islands poking out of the sea. These were like rest stops to relax and look for food.

I swooped down onto one island with a giant rock and perched upon it. I set the branch down in front of me, taking in a long breath to enjoy the scenery and coolness of the breeze.

A bit away from the rock, I saw a tree with plenty of nuts asking to be eaten. My eyes grew wide and my belly rumbled, so I set the branch down on the rock to enjoy these island nuts. They had such a delicious crunch and flavor, I almost wished I could bring some back to paradise.

Once full, I returned to the stone to retrieve my branch and be back on my way. As soon as I returned to where I set it, a shock ran through my body.

My heart started racing as I realized the branch was missing. I hopped around in a frenzy, searching in every direction, not leaving any stone unturned; but it was gone.

There were a few fruit trees about, but I couldn't just take a new branch, pretending it came from paradise. There were very strict guidelines for this journey and a biblical standard to meet.

Suddenly, a big shadow began hovering above me and

expanded like an ooze as the creature casting it descended to the ground right over my head. I looked up and saw him, this monstrous bird of prey. I could already tell he was no friend of paradise. I leapt out of his shadow as he touched the ground. The monster was holding my branch between his menacing smirk.

"Looking for something?" the bird of prey bullied.

"That's mine, give it back," I pled.

"This doesn't look or taste like any branch around these parts. Where are you from?"

"Paradise."

"Paradise huh? You ever see a bird like me around there?"

"No."

"No wonder. You haven't started running for your life."

"I'm not going anywhere without my branch."

"Why is this thing so important to you?

"None of your business."

"Then it must not be a big deal."

The bird of prey swung his neck and threw the branch over the ridge down to the sea below. I shot down the side of ridge, flying after the branch.

At all costs, I couldn't let it be swept away by the tide. As fast as I raced for the branch, I turned for a moment to see the bird of prey right behind me, his mouth agape and full of hope to swallow me whole.

"Come little one. I want to taste my first Bird of Paradise."

I reached the branch and quickly grabbed it in my beak right before we hit the water. I rose up, with my belly missing the sea's touch by inches, feeling the ocean's spray as I arced back upwards, trying to escape the bird of prey behind me.

"*Aww*, you caught your branch. It's too bad a dead bird has no use for such things."

This was the first predator I've ever encountered, and he was one with adequate experience picking flesh off bones. I've never been more scared in my life. The bird of prey couldn't tell though, because my nerves focused solely on flying at insane speed.

I tried to stay close to the water, hoping some rouge wave would slap the bird of prey out the sky. Then, when I approached any land sticking out the water, I would fly through any rocky hole or crevice to create an obstacle in the bird of prey's way.

I flew in long, winding curves, back and forth to tire the bird of prey out. I chewed a bit on my branch and was imbued with the endurance to fly for as long as the Bird of Prey pursued me.

My heart rate steadied. My blood stopped pumping so harshly; the fear was filtered out like dirty plasma. I knew I would escape unharmed. The more this thought made me smile, the more the distance between the bird of prey and I grew until finally, he became nothing more than a distant speck.

Whatever paradise was, this was surely it, the feeling of lucidity and freedom filling my body that you only experience after narrowly escaping death. It was the purest euphoria. God and Mother Bird were smiling down on me; for there would be no interference with destiny.

***

My only compass on this journey was my heart; which only presented obstacles before me so they may enlighten me. This included facing threats against my life, images that would break my heart, then moments that would repair it again.

Ahead, as I began to breach the ocean's fog, there was a beach spanning as wide as the eye could see. This was no small island for a bird to rest, this land mass was large enough to make Papua seem like any forgettable rock.

With so much room for opposing ideas and ways to live, this place was far from paradise. In paradise there was uniformity, a group-think to treat each other kindly. Think of it as a promise to take care of each other, and if that's too big of a promise to keep, perhaps humans don't deserve paradise after all. Human freedom is often nothing more than the freedom to be cruel.

I flew over the beach as the beautiful white sand glistened below me. All around, there were signs people once enjoyed this place. Balls and bicycles. Towels and surfboards. A summer oasis.

Soon, I realized these belongings that littered the beach were once held in human hands but somehow the humans they belonged to were nowhere to be found.

There were such things as toys, keys, photographs, and phones. I found a metal branch to perch upon and from there I overlooked this sad sight.

Closing my eyes and tapping into nature, I knew I was the only living bird around. It was just me and the tiny, hungry insect infestation.

Despite all this devastation, it was an extraordinarily beautiful day. The blue skies were a vivid cerulean. The sun shone bright. The clouds were fluffy, white, and peaceful. The trees would gently blow in the breeze and flourish in spite of sorrow's overwhelming presence.

I could take in a deep breath, my throat felt clear, the air felt soft, I looked around and knew what this place needed.

I began to sing and though I was a bit rusty, nature responded to my addition to its beauty. In one corner, a flower bloomed, in another, a happy bee came buzzing, the fruits and veggies glowed so ripe.

As I sang my prayer of hope, what I could only describe as a black metal bird came flying over. Just like the faceless ones that burned the forest, it was without a beak or eyes and made of the same shiny obsidian. It didn't flap its wings, but it displayed cognition as it hovered in front of me, examining me.

"Hello," I said to the faceless bird.

The sunlight shimmered against its obsidian skin. I wondered how it could see me without eyes.

"What is your name?" I asked.

It made some strange noises that sounded as though they were coming from inside the thing and not from any orifice.

Suddenly, in the distance, along came a swarm of them, approaching with a symphony of buzzing noise that filled me with a hot nausea.

I jumped off my metal branch and flew back toward the sea to save myself. The faceless birds were fast but didn't have the heart to push themselves faster than me.

Once I flew over the beach and crossed the shore, the faceless swarm stopped following me exactly where the land ended. They hovered in place, watching as I flew back on my way to find the people these beings most likely made vanish.

23

The Carola's Shade Song

Carola's Parotia is perhaps the most human of any Bird of Paradise. When the male dances, he holds a yellow leaf in his beak as if it were a rose to hand the female. No other Bird of Paradise uses a prop. I figure none ever thought of it.

They too like to lay low on the forest floor, clearing the ground of any off-putting objects, rocks, branches, or leaves. They make sure the grounds are well lit as well, with plenty of sun penetrating through the canopies above.

Then finally, a thick long branch spanning over the ground is necessary for the proper perching spot for a female. Once the place is tidy and the Parotia has its yellow leaf, the female lands on that branch to watch the show. The male does an intricate dance, wiggling his neck whiskers and staring at her with his uniquely yellow eyes.

Among the smallest of the Birds of Paradise, I had no trouble reaching the female after she rejected this poor fellow. She noticed a rogue pebble the poor bird overlooked when cleaning the dancing floor. Anyway, she had no trouble singing the Carola's Shade Song when I asked.

"So small a bird but with such beautiful eyes, like suns of honey dripping. The yellow rose, the yellow eyes, all combine for mellow

highs and mellow lows. Your dance is fancy, your whiskers wiggle,
no Parotia in Paradise is quite like you, my sweet Carola."

24

Among the Wreckage

One night a storm put my very soul on trial. The rains fell hard and long, never stopping - just like me. There was no land to shelter me in sight, seeing as my sight could only stretch about a meter ahead of me.

It was a struggle to keep my head up and not let the rain anchor me down into the ocean. With wings soaked and slowed to a lurching pace, I wormed my way through the thick grey sky, sheering through a wall of barbed water drops with every push forward.

Eventually, something hit me out the sky, it could've been a stone or flying fish, who knows but I went plummeting down, spinning in a vicious spiral until colliding with some hard surface in a divinely painful smash.

I thought I hit the water, but it was a massive bed of wood that miraculously broke my fall. As much as the sea wanted to swallow this wooden bed whole, it simply refused to be submerged. It bobbed up and down, as if God sent me a cradle.

I was completely winded, but still grateful. The only effort I could muster to express this gratitude was to keep my eyes open and upward to send an imaginary loving arrow up to heaven as thanks. I was hoping and praying I wouldn't perish. The trick was to keep my faith strong through the barrage.

***

The next morning, as the skies cleared and the storm was sent into hiding at the edges of the horizon, my eyes shed a tear upon the first sight of the revitalizing sun.

After about an hour of soaking in its healing rays and spitting out the rainwater in my belly, I was able to summon the strength to get to my feet and see for the first time I wasn't alone on this piece of wood.

A man with a long dirty beard, skin as brown as cured leather, and in a few tattered clothes was lying there. For a moment, I assumed he was dead until I saw his chest slowly rise up and down. He was breathing; my brother in surviving the storm.

Once I realized he was alive, I hopped onto his shoulder and started chirping into his ear. This proved to be completely useless until I peered down his ear canal and saw it was completely clogged. I slipped my beak inside and dug out the soft, squishy obstruction.

It was a giant glob of salty, wet, dark green algae. I spat the glob out and chirped deep into his ear till the sound echoed through his skull.

He stirred a bit but, still asleep, blindly swatted at me with his hand, nearly smacking me upside the head. I dodged his hand and furled my brow in frustration, I was going to have to wake him up with a few sharp pecks to wet my beak with his red sap to write with.

He snapped awake, his eyes advancing but his body retreating. He was afraid of me like I was some kind of evil omen.

The man screamed in foreign gibberish.

I sighed and rolled my eyes, wishing he would've

90

known English. As this man continued shouting at me in his strange tongue, I started writing with the blood he left on the tip of my beak. As soon as he saw me write, he shut up quite quickly. In awe, he began to read what I wrote on the wood.

"*English?*" he read, "Yes, I speak English. Are you friends with the dove?"

I responded with one of the most basic human expressions there was, a shrug.

"What do you want from me? Haven't you already taken enough?"

I began to write again.

"*Story?*" he read, "You want to hear my story?"

I nodded.

"Well, I've been through so much. I suppose it's nice to have someone to talk to, even if it is a bird."

I smiled and nodded, awaiting his story.

"I'm was born in the country of Pakistan. Have you heard of it?"

I shook my head.

"It is a beautiful country. A Muslim country. Next to India. Perhaps if I was born anywhere else, I would've fallen in love with a woman that wouldn't have turned my world upside down. I met her in India, where I lived before all these terrible things happened to the world."

Had I been a human, perhaps at this point I would've shown him a picture of my sweetheart.

"I was never treated well in India because of my religion. Still, even though I've always been an observant Muslim, I ended up falling in love with an Indian."

I was getting a bit confused why that would be strange, but he continued, mistaking the expression on my feathers.

"I was just as shocked as you are. Her name was Lily and she was the flower I planted in my heart."

I was in good company, that of a poet.

"We spent one summer two years ago falling more

deeply in love than we knew was possible. It was the sort of love that felt unquestionable. There was no doubt in my soul and none in her eyes. She was the moon in the night sky that guided my way."

Memories of Sarah sliced through my thoughts, almost pulling away my attention.

"Our families opposed our relationship. They thought we were spitting on our traditions. My parents wanted me to marry my own kind and her parents considered my kind the enemy. They fought with us day and night. Neither showed up to the wedding, but we didn't care. There was enough love between us to fill the empty spaces they left behind. We had two children, twin girls. Half of me, half of her, each of them."

Tears started streaming from his eyes. I felt mine trembling with wetness. His pain was so sharp, I could sense his past before he even told me. He lost everything.

All his spiritual and material wealth was stolen from him. He was as empty a shell as a person could be. I sensed this simply by the shape of his body, the musculature was of broken and crippled spirit.

"First my wife was taken. It was a slow process, this thing of loss. She was at home with me and had a burning fever, so high it seemed to scorch to her bones. I prayed to God every day until she was gone. Then I confronted God with such furious anger and pain, I cursed His name forever. He then repaid my spite by taking what was left of my family, my children, and leaving me all alone. I was already too hardened to save them by then. I couldn't even save myself, but as God would have it, my destiny was to live. It was a test, most likely, from the God I cursed. The next time I spoke to God, my anger was met with the sound of a bird's voice, that of a dove. I never heard a dove's voice before this, I heard one chirp but never speak."

I smiled, for I began to see how the mysteries with which God works were woven. Reality is a very elaborate and living story. It takes a storyteller to see the plot.

"The dove told me I would witness and experience horrible things. That of all the people I knew, I would suffer the most. The dove went on to say I must never lose my faith in God and must thank Him every day in prayer. I asked the dove what happens if I don't and the dove replied by telling me my family's souls would be at stake. They would watch me to make sure I prayed. Since the dove's instructions, I've prayed to God every day, and every day I've suffered; surviving disease, mutiny, storms, shipwreck, and drowning. I still wonder if that dove was sent by God or the devil. It could very well have been the devil playing a trick on another broken soul. I figure whoever sent that dove must've also sent you, so tell me, was it God or the devil?"

With his sap now dry on my beak, I wrote 'GOD' in big Hebrew letters any devout man ought to recognize no matter where he came from or what he spoke or believed in.

"Hebrew, ey? The devil would never dare utter that name for God. I believe you, little bird."

The waves gently bobbed the wooden bed up and down without disturbing us as we stared at each other in silence.

"Well…what did you come here to tell me?"

I grimaced.

"Is my family in heaven? Is this game over? Haven't I suffered enough? Are you here to bid me farewell? Why is it the dove could talk but you can't?"

I rolled my eyes and wrote, 'Where is everybody?'

"I bet you could write a whole book if you wanted, ey little bird? I can't speak for all humanity, but I was one of two captains of a fleet of survivors from India. We had two big boats worth of people. There was one of Hindus and the other, mine, were all Muslim. I don't know what happened to the Hindu boat, but I wouldn't be surprised if the storm destroyed their ship like it did mine. If they did survive, they must have starved by now. Given how long it's been since we left India and how much supplies they carried. My boat first hit that storm about a week ago. Then one especially monstrous wave destroyed the haul completely. It's a miracle I'm here with you."

He began to laugh.

"God is above all things a comedian first and a writer second. Can you imagine the sorry state of affairs when being stranded in the middle of the ocean with a bird on a piece of wood is considered a miracle? What does that make dinner and a drink then? Heaven?"

I shrugged.

"That's my story, little bird. What are you going to do with it?"

I wrote the words, 'New Land.'

"New land? As in a place to live? Where?"

'Papua,' I wrote.

"New Guinea? It's a beautiful island from what I've read. Say, you wouldn't happen to be one of those Birds of Paradise, would you?"

I bowed gracefully.

"You're not as colorful as some of the ones I've seen in pictures. That is why I asked."

I let out a deep sigh before moving on. 'Where can I find them?' I wrote.

"I'm not sure you'd want to. People can't survive this long by being kind, I'll guarantee you that. The only reason I'm still here is because I'm cursed."

'It's okay. They will learn to be kind,' I wrote.

"From who?"

'Me,' I wrote.

It was hard to believe he still had enough strength left in his body to laugh so hard. His back straightened and his whole chest expanded with every 'ha.'

His eyes filled with new life and his voice was cleared

of all its gravel. I'd have felt more embarrassed if I didn't notice the water swelling up behind him. We were being pulled back and upward. It seemed like we were being sucked into a big black shadow. As Ishmael laughed, a giant whale was usurping the seas to swallow us both. By the time the whale closed its mouth and we were inside it, Ishmael finally stopped laughing and opened his eyes.

"What on Earth...where are we?"

25

The Huon's Shade Song

This large Astrabia and its long, thick tail live on one of paradise's most isolated mountains. I found up there a young male ready to dance with a female by hanging upside down off a thick horizontal branch upon which both were perched.

From below, the male displays his beautiful green underbelly and then he touches the female with his beak. He's a very touchy-feely fellow for a male.

Sticking around to see if the male was winning her heart, the female stayed put and he started pecking at her nape. As you could have guessed, this male proved himself worthy.

Then, in what was the most unique dance I've seen thus far, the male hugged the female and pushed them both off their perch to free fall down the forest together.

The thrill seekers fearlessly shrieked through the fall, bracing the wind on their way. Before hitting the ground, they separated and flew off in opposite directions with, what I can only imagine, was all sorts of new spirit pumping through their veins.

As the female caught her breath, I approached her and made my usual pitch to get her to spill that sweet Shade Song verse. It turns out the Huon Astrabia's Shade Song is my personal favorite.

"Free Falling, little chick, you're free falling. Upside down look down below, the green of the forest is waiting for you. Once he takes you in his wings, you're gonna be free, free falling."

26

The Belly of the Bird

Sloshing around inside this smelly cavern, I could barely see anything but a light poking out from a hole in the creature's ceiling. This must have been the blow hole. I could hear the sounds of Ishmael's praying and smell the foul odors of this whale's interior.

"Please God, forgive me for all my transgressions. I never meant to stray from the path. I will always have faith in you God. You are supremely powerful. Thank you for always watching over me."

As Ishmael spoke, I realized I myself have never said a prayer for anything. I suppose because no one ever did so in front of me until now. This was as good a time to start as any, so I touched the tips of my wings together and bowed my head the way Ishmael did. I began to chirp.

"Dear God, please let me live to see paradise and Sarah again. I will lead the last humans on this Earth to their new home so long as you return me to mine."

Suddenly, the whale's sloshing began to take a reverse course. We began flowing forward toward the creature's mouth and not back toward its stomach.

"I did it. Prayer made the beast release us," Ishmael beamed with tears of joy in his foolish eyes.

The cavern's mouth opened and from it we emerged back into the world. The whale stuck its tongue out and held it there as its eyes rolled down toward us to give our odd pairing a good, long look.

"I never smelled anything worse in my life," sneered Ishmael.

The whale's eye rolled back up then down again and began drawing back its tongue, with us still on it, into its mouth.

The whale heard our prayers, gave us a chance, and realized we deserved digestion. If I were not to act at this moment, both myself and Ishmael were going to be eaten.

I flew off the creature's tongue just as its mouth shut on Ishmael, leaving him inside the beast as I flew up to its giant eye. I perched upon its nose and once the whale's attention fell on me, I began to dance, giving the whale my Rorschach test of feathers. In my black splotches, the whale saw his past, present, and future.

He saw all the things that brought us three to this very moment in which one of our lives was held in the belly of another. I saw the whale's pupil rattle around like a sparkling bobble until finally, his body began to rumble, and he hocked Ishmael out his blow hole in a giant glob of mucus.

Ishmael squealed as he flew through the sky and landed atop the whale's nose right beside me.

Here the two culprits were, side by side in the presence of this benevolent behemoth. I wished there was a way to say *thank you*, seeing as the big fellow let us live, but Ishmael had his own ideas.

"You big, fat tub of lard, who do you think you are? You nearly put an end to us both."

The whale didn't pay him any mind though. He felt badly for me, imagining what I must've been through with Ishmael as my only company.

Seeing as our piece of wood was gone, Ishmael and I

had no hope to travel. So, dazzling the whale again with my beautiful plumage, I flew up into the sky and led the whale to swim with half his body poking above the water so Ishmael wouldn't drown.

We journeyed this way, the three of us, like no human could've ever thought was possible until we found a stretch of dry land for Ishmael's feet to walk upon.

This felt far from fantasy but rather, this was a showing of the bonds between all species in nature. That when love is shown, it is always reciprocated. This is a natural law, if only humans would identify themselves as nature.

***

The whale took us to some seaside village, a place that must've once been very relaxing for a human to vacation. Just like the last island I toured; this one had all sorts of litter lying about the beach. Sensing no danger, this was as far as the whale was willing to take us. As the whale submerged back below the ocean's surface, Ishmael and I walked up the shore onto the sand. He didn't say much but I could tell he was bothered.

"The whale took us to Goa. This was a mistake. If I stay here long, I will not survive."

I jumped up on his shoulder and wrote a question mark on his neck without breaking his skin. He was able to read solely through touch.

"Why? Because once a handful of us survived the cataclysm, the mad rulers responsible sent machine men to guard the land and attack any intruders."

We slogged through the sand, walking along the shore's very edge, avoiding the mainland as much as possible.

"These machine men patrol the cities. Anyone they see alive is quickly removed, and they have eyes everywhere."

I again wrote a question mark on his neck. The peck of

the dot below the curve, sent a bolt of frustration through him.

"What don't you get? The fall of mankind was not a naturally occurring event. Humanity caused its own demise. The masterminds of this great catastrophe that are still alive today lost their humanity long ago. They saw us as a necessary sacrifice to make a race of *super men*. Perhaps they saw themselves as angels, ascending Jacob's ladder; angels of death they are."

We kept walking down the shore until we reached a point where the natural land stopped, and the paved road began.

"We can either go backward to the other end of the shore or we can continue. Either way, we have to find a boat."

I pointed forward and Ishmael already knew this was our only option. He took a long sigh because he knew as soon as we left the sand, they were going to come for us.

"Do not make a sound. The least we could do is be silent."

We snuck onto the pier, hiding behind the shops, restaurants, tables, and fair that humans used to frequent. My eyes followed his and every time he looked up, it was at a different black box with a glass face, all following our movements.

I heard the familiar hum of faceless birds and saw Ishmael start to sprint. He ran for his life, dipping under or behind every object as if certain death was right on our tail. I had to jump off his shoulder and fly behind him.

"If I perish, you have to keep going. Find others, they're out there. Don't pay any mind to whatever bad things I said about them. If they suffered, they learned," Ishmael begged of me in between his heavy pants.

Ishmael kept running until we reached the other end of the pier from which he could step back onto the beach. At this point, the hum of the faceless bird grew loud enough to nauseate a human.

I suddenly felt feverish, even a bit bloated. I had to get away. I flew up and out over the water so I could watch the faceless bird chase Ishmael. At the end of the beach, there was a little marina. A few boats were tied to a wooden dock there.

As soon as he saw this dock, he must've been just as excited as I was because now there was hope he wouldn't perish. Once he reached the dock, he quickly started untying the nearest motorboat.

Then appeared a form from the past, a faceless one arrived at the mouth of the marina. It was there to remove that which was not meant to be present.

Compared to Ishmael, this faceless one was twice his size. Unlike humans made of flesh, faceless ones looked the same no matter where they came from. It seemed as though the two faceless beings, the bird and the one, were friends the same way I was with Ishmael.

Ishmael finished freeing the motorboat and hopped inside. The faceless one ran over to him and appeared to raise his hand over Ishmael's face. In an instance, Ishmael fell to the faceless one's feet.

I wanted to stay behind and see if Ishmael would survive but, within seconds, the faceless bird came after me.

I escaped by flying back toward the ocean but couldn't look back to see what became of my new friend and the only human I found on my journey.

I kept asking myself why God would allow this to happen but never coming up with an answer. I felt lost - like a failure because the Mother Bird told me to find humans and protect them, but I couldn't protect Ishmael.

So, upset, my flight away from the island was marred with a mind full of questions. I asked myself how humanity could do this to each other. How could those with power be so cruel to those without.

The greatest question I asked was this: 'Under the weight of life's unsureness, will humanity relinquish their

responsibility to take care of their fellow man?' The answer
can only be no.

27

The Blue's Shade Song

Every Bird of Paradise is envious of the Blue. There's a long list of reasons why: their colors, their style, their rarity. Even the females have beautiful blue plumage. It's not fair.

Personally, they were the one bird I've been trying to avoid. They have this incredible display. I've seen it. It's special, but so what? That doesn't mean they can walk around with their beaks up in the air like the rest of us are beneath them.

First, the male perches on a horizontal branch and puffs out his blue flanking feathers like an apron. He falls back, tail-first to hang upside down on the branch with his beak pointing upwards as the female stands directly over him.

Now, to top it all off, as if this wasn't enough, the Blue sings with the most powerful pulsating song. When you hear it, you drop everything, it's the most alluring sound in this entire forest. It's the sound of paradise itself...*those little show-offs*.

I didn't even bother trying to eavesdrop on the *love birds* getting to know each other. I didn't care to anger myself. I stumbled upon a few elusive female Blue Birds of Paradise just milling about their habitat.

"Excuse me, you're a Blue Bird of Paradise, aren't you?" I asked one.

"Are you blind or just stupid?" she replied.

"Stupid. I'm going around collecting the Shade Songs of every Bird of Paradise."

"Who do you think you are? Asking for my precious Shade Song...."

"Just a humble writer."

Suddenly, the pulsating sound of the male Blue Bird of Paradise's song rang through the forest. Every other female flew away to see the male's attempt but this one I was bothering.

"Just stay. You've seen it before," I pleaded with her.

"But don't you want to see the incredible display of a Blue Bird of Paradise?"

"No. I don't care."

"You're not even a little bit curious?"

"I'm just here for the Shade Song."

Shocked I wasn't impressed, she paused to gather her thoughts.

"I didn't think it was possible for another bird to be completely indifferent to us."

"Please, just sing."

She stared at me blankly, her world turned upside down.

"The bluest eyes, the bluest plumage, below the sky but above your dancing. She hears the song of paradise, pulsating through the forest. Of all the birds and all the songs this forest has to offer, no other bird could possibly be so lucky of a dance partner. Few in numbers, so shinning are you, chick of paradise's blueness."

28

Death Is Simply a Return

Does all the loss that occurred lessen one's faith in God or strengthen it? If you ask yourself why or how God would be capable of committing such violence, then you might lose your faith completely. If you ask yourself where all these souls go after this life, it simply feels wrong that the answer be nowhere at all. When death is so prevalent, the living can feel the other side pulling at them too. Where exactly does a spirit go then? Heaven? Does a Bird of Paradise believe in heaven? Yes. And it took the loss of millions to make me know this truth.

After he faced a faceless one, I assumed Ishmael's soul floated up the sky and returned to the holy glow. Each living being here on Earth has a small sliver of that holy glow in them. It's possible to sin enough that you dampen the holy glow inside you and eventually put out its light completely. For the most part though, the living keep their holy glow until material death so that piece may return to the whole it came from.

***

The skies were clear as a dream, without a single cloud.

Then I saw it; a ship, long and metal, in the distance. My eyes filled with saltwater and those tears fell to marry the drops in the ocean. When I reached the boat, I saw it was missing the entire rear half of its haul; like it was sawed in half by a shark bite. The ship seemed empty, cold, and devoid of life. I flew around the ship and saw Hebrew letters written on its side that read '*Libertine.*'

Suddenly, I saw a plume of smoke rising up from the deck's broken edge and waddled my way over, curious as to where the fire was coming from.

As I peeked over the side of the deck, I saw nothing but water. After flying down and inspecting the interior level beneath the deck, I saw a human smoking a cigarette. He and his cigarette were Israeli.

The cigarette's smoke lifted up to the ceiling then rolled out the breached opening of the boat. The Israeli sat and watched the ocean from out the broken haul, holding a knife limply in his hand. His eyes were fixed upon the water as it rolled us forward in a dumb drift.

A Bird of Paradise in the middle of this nowhere seemed like no shock to him, he didn't even direct his smoke elsewhere in courtesy of me.

Mentally, it seemed to me that he had checked out. The only thing I could do to grab his attention seemed to be to snap the cigarette out of his mouth. Furious, he tried to slash me open with his knife while shouting at me in Hebrew.

"Stupid pigeon!"

I used the cigarette to write my displeasure with the Israeli in black ash on the metal floor. I simply wrote 'Pigeon?' in Hebrew.

Now that I had his full attention, he shut up immediately, completely perplexed. The Israeli proved to be incredibly intelligent, speaking two steps ahead in the conversation.

"I'm sorry. I can see now you are not a pigeon. No

pigeon could ever learn to write. Your brain must be a little bigger and judging by your plumage, you must be a Bird of Paradise. What you would be doing all the way out here? I couldn't possibly imagine."

The language of this answer enchanted me. When he spoke, it felt like music. I was certain he was a writer of some sort. I wrote 'Are you a writer?' with the cigarette's ashen tip.

"Me? No, there's no use to write. Even before all this happened, no one was reading a word anyone had to say. They'd read the headline of an article on their phone, but never a new book. Maybe they'd check out an old book they heard was brilliant, but even that was rare. Are you a writer?"

I couldn't believe he asked me. How could he have possibly known? I replied 'Yes' and upon finishing the 's,' the cigarette ran out of ash to write with.

"Here," he said as he handed me a perfectly sized pencil. I took the pencil in my beak and bowed to him in thanks.

"Then again, no bird ever wrote a book. I would read a book written by an animal."

I wrote 'Thanks.'

"Say, since you're a writer and all, why don't you write down your story for me. I'm incredibly curious as to what you're doing here."

As ecstatic as I was about the idea, I wasn't sure how to summarize everything in a short period of time. I simply wrote, 'But time?' knowing he would understand what I meant.

"We've got all the time in the world. There's still some food left aboard if you'd like some. I'm not hungry myself. I'd prefer just to smoke and watch the waves. I'm still in shock, you see."

I nodded and flew away to another part of the floor where I had enough room to write my story.

"My name's Isaac by the way," said the Israeli.

When Isaac finished reading what I wrote and wiped his eyes dry, he turned to me and said, "You know, Jews and Arabs once had a great deal of hatred toward each other. Now though..." he lifted his head up, as if looking up to the sky to make sure God could see and hear him say this, "Now, I feel no hatred toward anyone at all. How could I? After what I went through? There are no more borders or holy lands," he then turned to me, "with the exception of this place you call paradise, I suppose."

Isaac stood up from the kneeling position he took to read my story then sat down next to me at the floor's edge. He lit another cigarette to talk to me face to face, "You know, this rings awfully familiar. Everything you're out here to do. It's almost like we're reliving the Bible."

I shrugged then nodded.

"That would make me a key figure in the story then. Especially if we found these people you were looking for together. Abraham, I will do everything in my power to help you under one condition."

I paused and kicked at him, awaiting his proposition.

"When you write this story, I want you to give me the title of 'prophet.' All the important minor characters in the Bible were prophets. People still remember them. You make me 'Isaac the Prophet' and I will find the people still out there."

I simply wrote, 'Deal.'

"Also, if you're going to write this story. You need to know the entire Bible as well I do. Would you like me to recite it for you in its entirety?"

I nodded.

Isaac smiled and closed his eyes, "Treat others the way you would like to be treated. That is the whole of the law. The rest is explanation." He smiled and opened his eyes.

He picked me up from the ground and put me on his shoulder. I don't understand why humans love keeping birds on their shoulders so much.

"I have a compass, map, food, water, and one lifeboat left. I wasn't planning on using it, though. To be honest, I was about to do something terrible to myself before you showed up," he admitted, visibly conflicted within.

I was surprised such a smart and decent man would be willing to do something so drastic as what I assumed.

"I can tell what you're thinking, Abraham. You don't have to waste your time and write it. I was at a point where life had lost its beauty. What we pretend to be beautiful now is an insult to how life is meant to be lived. Life used to be so incredibly beautiful. I'd sooner live just to remember the past before I act like this present is tolerable, let alone beautiful. We shouldn't fear death just because we know nothing about it. We should accept it. I trust in reality's sense of irony more than anything. The irony with which the story of reality plays out is the closest thing to proof of God I can think of. Narrative logic and poetic justice in life are kinds of evidence for the existence of metaphysics. That's why it's so funny you came around when you did."

***

We pulleyed down the side of the *Libertine* in the last remaining lifeboat. Isaac inspected the map as he lit a cigarette to smoke.

"Wish we knew exactly where we were," he commiserated.

I took the pencil and began writing on the map. Once I found India, I drew a circle around Goa then an arrow toward the ocean where I suspected we were.

"We're off the coast of Goa? Is that where you and Ishmael were taken by the whale?"

I nodded.

"Then there are a few options where we could go. How about Africa? That's where humanity originated anyway. If you'd like to see the Garden of Eden, it would only make sense if it were somewhere there."

Isaac checked his compass to make sure we would venture westward and then we were off in search of anyone that gravitated toward humanity's birthplace with us. I could see what Isaac meant now, the irony in reality. We were being pulled by something to seek humanity's birthplace in the time of humanity's death. We were sure there would be others drawn by this force too.

Because the journey was long and boring by boat, the two of us had to find ways to entertain each other. Isaac brought along a notepad for me and asked me to write a story every day for him to recite. The only problem was, they ended up all being variations of the same plot.

"There was once a bird named Sarah," he began before putting the notepad down and glaring at me. "How will you ever be a great writer if you only write about her? People write about all kinds of things, science fiction, history, fantasy - you name it. Sarah might be nice but, in the end, why should I care?"

I could've strangled him at that moment. Instead, I furiously hopped up and pecked him in the center of his forehead.

"What the heck," Isaac yelped. "That hurt."

To retaliate, he took my only pencil, broke it in half, then threw both pieces into the ocean.

"There. I shut you up for good now."

I was breathing so hard, my body puffed-up to twice its size. Isaac knew he was in for a fight and raised both his fists. "I'm not too proud to knock a bird out cold."

I was boiling over with rage, but reconsidering my desire to destroy him, I realized fighting was not the worst thing I could do to Isaac. I simply started flying away.

"Where are you going?" Isaac stood up in the boat, "You're going to strand me out in the middle of the ocean to rot? After all I did for you? Come back down here and face me."

I flew far enough away to bring Isaac's heart to the brink of breaking before returning to the boat to find him in tears.

"Please don't ever scare me like that again," Isaac begged, sucking up his snot.

***

One shinning morning, as the both of us slept, we were jolted out of our gentle dreaming by the loud, booming call of some approaching siren.

When Isaac and I jumped up and opened our eyes, we saw it in the distance; a sailboat off the coast of what had to be Africa. The crew was small, black, and smiling at us, waving jubilantly.

I grabbed the branch and took flight as Isaac steered the lifeboat in the direction of my flying.

As I reached the boat and perched upon the deck's railing to greet these humans, I was met by a dozen black men and women, happier to see me than any humans before them. One of them walked up to me with a happy glow on his face.

"Hello, my name is Captain Obu. This is my ship, the *Lonely Palm*. And these are my crew."

"Hello," his crew happily greeted me, all together.

He knew to talk to me as if he heard from someone I was coming. I flew over to him with the branch and laid it at his feet. He picked it up and examined it closely then tasted it with a nibble.

"Where did you get this branch?"

I flew out to sea to guide him toward Papua as Isaac's

lifeboat approached the *Lonely Palm*.

"Hello," said Isaac.

Captain Obu waved back at him, "Greetings."

"That bird is named Abraham. He understands English. He came all the way from Papua, New Guinea to find you. According to Abraham, Papua is the only place humans can live in peace anymore. That's where the branch is from. He wants to take us there."

Captain Obu nodded, absorbing the life-altering gravity of this information. He turned to his crew and with a smile said, "We are saved."

29

The Red's Shade Song

A bit off the mainland is an island where the Red Bird of Paradise lives in isolation. Paradise's effects stretch far across these islands, fostering the creation of a very splendid specimen.

Above each eye are shiny green feathers which stand straight up in the presence of females. The Red is named after the bright red plumes that remain stiffly curved even when they invert upside-down during their dances.

The species' final distinction is the two tiny ribbon like feathers sticking out the bird's behind that form the shape of a heart during a dance.

Out of curiosity, I snuck up on a male trying to grab a female's attention. You see, the Red is just as rare as the Blue, but is completely humble about it. They don't beg for your attention; they earn it by being shy and thus elusive.

When the female arrived on the branch and the male swooped downward, his curved feathers appeared like the sharp crescents of a blood moon. I could see her eyes swivel in mirror motion to him.

She was completely transfixed and, as his feathers jostled below her, the ribbons made the shape of a heart. This bird inspired in me a new understanding of love. As humble as he was, love was loudly pouring out of every feather. He was unashamed and genuine about it.

When I caught up with a female to introduce myself, she stayed silent the entire time, as if any interaction with a different species was improper or scary. When I asked for her Shade Song verse, she sang without making a fuss, hoping after I heard what I wanted to, I'd leave her be.

"The red feathers of the red moon hook beneath the beautiful bird's eyes. They hold her and they sing to her for she is all that's ever mattered. No time to laugh, no time to cry, no heart to gloat, a beautiful bird must be shy. The green of your eyes, the green of your feathers, and the red of your beautiful tail, they all make that heart shape more humbling."

30

An Africa, a Jew and
a Bird Walk Onto a Boat

When Isaac boarded the *Lonely Palm* and I returned to my perch upon the boat's rail. Isaac acted as ambassador to paradise for me to these beautiful humans. "Where did you all come from?"

"Ethiopia."

"Ah, I am from Israel. We are brothers."

"We would be brothers no matter where we came from. Too much blood has been spilt not to recognize the familial bonds between all humans," said Captain Obu.

"Agreed. So, will you follow us?" Isaac asked.

"To Papua, New Guinea?"

"Yes."

"Is it nice?" Obu asked.

"It's paradise."

"Well, when you put it that way…sure, why not?"

Following my lead, Captain Obu sailed the *Lonely Palm* back toward Papua. While the sun was up, the sails and my wings were up.

When the sun was down, we all came together to celebrate and love each other. I would regale the humans with stories every night. Then they would dance, sing, and play music on various African instruments. They would share their food with us and Isaac would share Israeli food with them. It became a cross-continental buffet of foods I never tasted and sounds I never heard; all expanding my senses far beyond the limits of your average Bird of Paradise.

Isaac even met a girl aboard the ship, a beautiful African woman with big curly hair like his named Delilah. We were one big family, not competing with each other.

Already the humans were picking up after Birds of Paradise. I knew my work ahead would be a breeze. The teachings of nature were inherent in people after all. It's a shame it takes suffering to refresh their memories.

We sailed for weeks on end. Isaac was tracking our movements on the map and surmised we were reaching the Western coast of Australia.

Soon, another boat began approaching us with twice the size, but half the crew. The crew of this big behemoth were all white, male Aussies. There was not a single aboriginal or woman in the bunch.

The ship's captain examined our odd lot through his telescope, not sure of how to best bully us out of his way. Replacing his telescope with a megaphone, the captain began to bark at us. "Hello, my name is Captain Skullgrass. I come in peace. Come aboard the *Glossy Pearl*. We're a welcoming crew of fun-loving lads."

As we drew in closer, Isaac looked at Captain Obu, curiously, "What do you think, Captain?" he asked.

"I know better than to trust just anyone."

"Really? But you trusted me."

"You and I are both children of Zion…but if you keep questioning my instincts, perhaps I'll change my mind about you."

"So, what do you suggest? We just blow him off?"

"We should sail past them and not say a word."

"That's so rude they might try to pirate our ship simply out of spite."

"Maybe so, but if we step onto that boat, we will never return."

"There has to be a way to test them."

"Send the bird," Captain Obu suggested.

I turned to Captain Obu and groaned. If I could get close enough to get a feel for them, I would know whether they were worthy of paradise.

"What do you say, Abraham?" Isaac asked me.

I took off for the *Glossy Pearl*. Once I perched upon the deck railing, Captain Skullgrass lowered his megaphone and turned to a few blokes beside him. "Ay, looks like we won't starve after all." Eyeing me he joked, "A little snack before we eat all the food on their ship."

Captain Obu was right, their screwball crew of scoundrels were only interested in our booty. Within moments, one of the three grabbed a net as they all came creeping closer, trying to snatch me up.

I quickly fell back off the railing and flew to our boat. When I returned to Captain Obu and Isaac, I shook my head and they both understood it was best to avoid the *Glossy Pearl*.

As we sailed past them, veering farther and farther away with every inch, Captain Skullgrass began to worry. "Hey, where are you going? What's wrong? You don't think we're friendly?"

We paid him no mind and just kept going.

"I told you we come in peace. Don't you believe us? Are you calling me a liar?"

"Here we go, no respect," said Captain Obu, shaking his head.

"You were right. I was wrong," Isaac admitted.

"Alright, I suppose I'll come to you," Captain Skullgrass lamented as the *Glossy Pearl* started following our sailboat.

The *Lonely Palm* was fast, but the *Glossy Pearl* was equipped with enough engines to force the behemoth forward against the waves to close in on us like a great white does a tuna. Gaining on us, I could see Captain Obu quickly losing his cool as hysteria began to infect the crew.

Then out of nowhere, the *Glossy Pearl* was struck by a bigger behemoth under the water's surface. Ramming it with a stiff shoulder, nearly knocking it over completely, a great wave was created by the clashing of marine flesh against the boat's heavy haul.

Emerging from the water after hitting the *Glossy Pearl* was the great whale that swallowed Ishmael and me.

The *Glossy Pearl* tipped from side to side, as the waves beneath it tossed it around as if it was light as a feather. It nearly careened off its axis before the whale saved the ship from tipping over completely by pressing against its side till it straightened back on its axis. The whale didn't want to see anyone get hurt; not us, not them.

To ensure our passage home was safe, the whale sat before the *Glossy Pearl* as still as a wall, blocking Captain Skullgrass from following us to paradise. I don't know what became of the Captain and even though I couldn't let him make a home in paradise, I truly do hope he's okay and learned the error of his ways.

The rest of the trip was rather calm from here on. The only bump in the water came about one sunset after we already saw Papua in the distance. A lone boat was bobbing in the waves with apparently no one on board.

"If anyone is on it, they must be dead," Captain Obu said.

I decided to check for myself. A certain warmth in my heart drew me to the boat as I flew its way. When I looked down, hoping to see a human being in the boat, I found two; a brown man and a white woman, both lying face down.

I pecked the back of the brown head and eventually he

stirred awake, grumbling in Arabic. It was Ishmael. A jolt of joy and accomplishment rushed through my body like a happy shock.

Ishmael sat up, still very much alive and, again, tried to swat me out of the sky before he opened his eyes to see we were reunited.

"That you, little bird?"

I smiled and started dancing in front of him.

"That's amazing. Can you believe it? I told you God wouldn't let me perish. Sheesh. You know times are strange when it's easier to predict the future than describe the present. Did you come with that whale? Wherever I am, he isn't far behind. I swear I've seen him five times since we got swallowed."

Ishmael looked up to see Captain Obu's sailboat approaching us.

"You found people! What a coincidence, so did I." Ishmael nudged the woman awake and she sat up to see me eyeing her.

"Where are we?" she asked as she rose.

"Karen, this is Abraham. He's a bird that knows how to write in English. Abraham, this is Karen. She saved my life."

I flew over to Karen and bowed to her. She glid her finger down my back, melting me. I could sense she had a very lovely heart already.

"If you're wondering how I survived Goa, I played possum then kicked that robot's feet from under him. He fell into the water and short circuited. Then I sailed away on my escape. A few days later, I found myself out of food until I ran into Karen here on this boat and she took me in."

I pointed to Papua's mainland behind them in the distance.

"Is that Papua?"

I nodded and Ishmael slapped himself against the

forehead, laughing to high heaven.

"What a joke. We could've found it without you, Abraham."

As Captain Obu's boat reached Ishmael's, the Captain called out to him.

"You are welcome onto my boat, but your woman is not."

"I am not *his* woman," Karen fumed.

I flew over to the Captain, and glared at him so furiously, he couldn't mistake the gesture.

"What?" he shrugged to me, "I will not share my boat with her."

"What did I ever do to you?" she asked him.

"It's what I think you will do…eventually. If you are coming to paradise, my crew will have to head back."

"Are you crazy?" Isaac asked the Captain.

"No. Crazy is doing the same things and expecting different results. I will not make the same mistakes of my ancestors."

I flew over to Ishmael's boat to signify I was taking Karen and Ishmael's side.

"So, you chose her? Fine." Captain Obu then turned to Isaac, "You go with them too."

"I was planning on it," Isaac said, while shaking his head.

Isaac jumped out of Captain Obu's boat, swam over to Ishmael's and, upon reaching the side, stuck his hand out for us to grab and pull him out of the water.

"What is your accent?" Ishmael asked Isaac.

"Israeli," Isaac said.

Ishmael hesitated pulling Isaac into his boat, smiling at him deviously. Isaac couldn't stay afloat much longer. He started to slap the water to stop himself from sinking.

"What your problem?" Karen asked Ishmael as she attempted to pull Isaac into the boat all by herself.

Ishmael continued without lifting a finger to help. "After everything your people did to mine. You think I'd let you in my boat?"

As Karen pulled and pulled, she only ended up falling forward into the water with Isaac; sending a wave of laughter through Captain Obu's crew. I was incensed. First, Ishmael got a good pecking. Then I flew back and dealt one to Captain Obu.

"You stupid little bird, you sent us out here for nothing," Obu whined as he tried to slap me out of the air.

Just as he started shouting at me, Delilah jumped overboard and swam over to Isaac to help him and Karen.

As Isaac floated beside Ishmael's boat with the two women, he tried to make the case for peace to him. "Listen, no individual represents the entire history of their people. The only people any of us represent now are the people still alive. How do *you* make us look if you don't let us board your ship?"

Ishmael crossed his arms over his chest. "I like this guy," Captain Obu said, sending his respect to Ishmael.

"What happened to us being brothers?" Isaac asked Captain Obu.

"You chose her over me, brother," Captain Obu reasoned.

"Why does it even matter what group she was born into? It's what's in her head and heart that matters."

"It matters to me." Obu wouldn't budge.

"Don't you get it?" Karen finally spouted, "I didn't care whether Ishmael was Pakistani, Indian, Muslim, or Jew...*he was hungry*. If I didn't feed him, he would've perished. Far too many people have perished already. Why are we alive other than to help each other live?"

"You need to shut up, little girl," the Captain lost his cool and decided he didn't want to hear any more of it.

Suddenly, everyone started bickering between them

until Isaac tried to pull himself up into Ishmael's boat all by himself and ended up flipping it over completely, sending Ishmael into the water too.

Everyone swam back to the *Lonely Palm* and tried getting in as Captain Obu kicked at them. I did my best to fluster the Captain, but it was no use, he ended up grabbing me and clutching me in his fist with a firm squeeze. "If you keep asking me to help someone intent on harming me, I will have to harm you," Obu said as he clenched his fist tighter around me, squeezing the breath out of my body.

Suddenly, coming to my rescue from the sky was a beautiful brown Superb bird with a beak so sharp it stabbed into the Captain's nose and sent him to the ground, yelping in pain. Everyone was shocked into silence and, while Obu's crew was busy aiding him, everyone in the water climbed up onto the *Lonely Palm* to join the crew.

"I've been hit. Something shot me in my nose. I can't smell," Obu scrambled and screamed.

As everyone turned to see what it was that attacked Captain Obu, they found me in a tight embrace with my sweetheart. They could not hold any anger toward Sarah after seeing us show such adoration toward each other.

All our longing was finally turned to pure joy in that moment. Our tears, coos, and nuzzles sent melting waves of empathy into every human there to witness it. They no longer remembered why they were fighting amongst each other.

Obu sat up to see Sarah beside me with drops of his blood at her feet. "It was a bird that attacked me? Grab it before it escapes," Obu demanded.

The *Lonely Palm's* crew would not comply, they became privy to the future of humanity that Obu simply could not see.

"No," said Delilah, "We will not hurt any more creatures, bird or human. None of us wish to harm any others and if you ask us to again then when we arrive on paradise, you can go your own way and be all by yourself. This crew and ship are no longer yours, Obu."

"Really? Then I suppose you'll need a new Captain." Obu protested.

"If that's the case then I choose Abraham. He is more than man enough for the job," Delilah said.

They all had a good giggle at the idea, but were still all in agreement. I had the sensitivity, heart, and wisdom to lead these humans to paradise.

31

The Emperor's Shade Song

In the world of Paradise, there are Kings but then there are Emperors. You won't find them lording it over the forest floors or the mountain tops. They like to spend their days in between - in range of both kingdoms, high and low. With glowing green feathers on its head and white fluffy plumes on either side of its body, like so many other birds, the Emperor enjoys hanging upside down as the female perches above him, between his feet, in scrutiny of royalty.

One female stood over a flirting Emperor Bird of Paradise with such an expression of boredom on her face I was able to fly up to her in the middle of the dance and just ask for her to leave with me so she could sing me her Shade Song.

A Bird of Paradise has to learn they cannot rest on their laurels, whether they be Kings or Emperors, a bad display won't win them a pauper for a mate. The female and I found some privacy for her to sing.

"Of royal highs and royal lows, the mountain's middle we call home. Green and white you'll hang your head as if you had a crown of feathers, but rest assured the day will come that no crown can take the place of a romantic heart's courtship."

32

We Arrive

The view with which they were greeted was awesome enough to break any spells these humans had cast upon them to make them hate each other. The glory of nature shined with a sacred light that imbued every rib of every leaf and every wrinkle in every tree.

This beauty was not lost upon these humans and even though they went through terrible struggles, the lot of them still thirsted for slices of heaven like this.

The moment they stepped foot on the soil sent a silent shockwave through the entire forest and just like when Sarah first sang the Shade Song, every Bird of Paradise gathered to welcome the refugees.

Already, there were murmurs among them as they watched Sarah and I escort the pack of humans through the forest.

"Abraham is back."

"Those must be the humans he saved."

"Thank goodness, Sarah was worried sick."

"He looks awful. I can't imagine what he's been through."

Once we arrived in a forest clearing with all the birds perched in the branches above and around us, I took the moment to address the community.

"Paradise, I have finally returned to you. These are the humans the Mother Bird wanted me to save. They are tired, hungry, and ready to learn our ways."

A wind blew through the forest clearing and carried a swell of dust that began forming the body of our Mother Bird. As the wind died down, our Mother came to life right before our eyes. The humans were even more astonished than the birds.

"It's bird magic," yelped Captain Obu in shock.

"That must be Noah's dove," Isaac said.

"Finally. You have returned to me," Ishmael said to the Mother Bird.

The Mother Bird walked up to Sarah and I first. Smiling at us both, she kissed her on the cheek, then me.

"Welcome back, dear," she said in the sweetest, most motherly tone before turning from us to the humans to see who I brought to her. "Ah, Ishmael. Good to see you," the Mother Bird recognized him.

"Where are my wife and children, dove?" Ishmael asked her.

"In heaven now. Their spirits are all around us, all those we loved and lost are the lifeblood flowing through this sacred place. Do you feel them?"

"I don't know," Ishmael said.

"Close your eyes and breathe deeply. Then tell me what you sense."

Ishmael did just as the Mother Bird instructed him, for everything she told him came true. He prayed every day and survived every terror. He closed his eyes and breathed. A shudder ran down his back that sent his whole body into shambles. He began to sob revelatory tears. He smelled his wife; he heard his children's breathing. His crying symbolized to him the end of a long and exhausting journey.

"Thank you. Thank you so much, little dove," Ishmael

cried.

Karen walked over to him and rubbed his back, comforting him through the agonizing relief.

"You should all consider yourselves to be incredibly lucky."

"We do," Karen said to the Mother Bird; which was met by Captain Obu's jeering.

"You should consider yourself the luckiest of all, Obu," the Mother Bird spoke.

"Really? You watch. This little experiment will fail soon enough. There could have been unity among us. Now she's poisoned any chance of that."

"You're the poison, Obu," the Mother Bird shook her head.

"I am trying to keep it pure."

"Then go your own way. Be pure in isolation. You're not doing anyone any good if you stay."

I approached the Mother Bird. "Please Mother Bird, let him stay. He is wrong, hardheaded, sometimes he's even cruel; but he can learn."

"Then you will have to deal with his hatred. Good luck. Hatred will weigh down the entire process."

"I will carry it none the less."

"You're lucky Abraham has shown you mercy, Obu," the Mother Bird told him, to which the Captain merely laughed.

"I'm surprised you know so little about human nature," said the Captain.

"Human nature lost you the human world. Now that you're in the world of birds, we expect you to learn something about birdly nature."

The Captain had nothing to say but Isaac stepped forward to make a point. "Yes, there is much we humans can learn from you birds, but correct me if I'm wrong, Abraham wanted you birds to learn from us humans too, did he not?"

"Yes. There is much we want to learn."

"Well, there is a reason humanity was chosen to lord over the animals and a reason you animals accept us lording over you."

"What reasons are those?"

"Humans think for themselves. We are not bound to act in any uniform way. We lack cohesion, but we are free."

"What good is freedom if you can't get along?"

"Without freedom we could garden the Earth, but we wouldn't enjoy it."

"As a bird, we know a little bit more about freedom than man. We roam the sky. If you want to be completely free, then leave this place and be free and alone. If you stay here, you're going to be committed to nature."

33

Life in Paradise

The Mother Bird led us on a long march through the forest. Every step the humans took, the birds followed in a slow flutter above them in the canopies. We arrived at my cabin and stopped.

"You had a cabin ready for us?" Isaac asked.

No. This is Abraham's cabin; unless he wants to lend it to you," the Mother Bird replied.

"I need my privacy to write," I told the Mother Bird.

"Abraham says *no*," the Mother Bird relayed to the humans. "So, you will set up camp here. Make your homes and beds with whatever you can find."

"Does anyone know how to build a shelter?" Isaac asked.

Everyone turned their heads to Captain Obu.

He sighed and resigned himself to his duty. "Follow me."

Obu led the men in collecting the necessary materials; be they the flanks of wood he chopped off the trees with his machete or the vines he stripped down to string required to tie the structures together. After a long day of work, makeshift shelters were made to cover the humans from the Papua rain. Our rains are not a brutal expression of the elements. They fall upon human heads with a gentle jungle kiss.

As the humans spent the night sleeping after a tiresome introduction to paradise, I was in my cabin writing my book. It had been so long since I visited my manuscript, I started noticing all the flaws I left behind in the first round of writing. I was so full of memories, feelings, and inspiration. I let it spill onto the pages in furious spells of scribbling that plagued me until sunrise.

That morning, on little sleep, I woke the humans with a song that rang through the forest and summoned the birds to the human's first lesson in the ways of paradise. The humans arose from their slumbers, some alone, others not, and the first to make a peep was Ishmael. "Is there anything to eat around here? Do you birds drink coffee?"

"I nodded at Ishmael then flew over to lead him to food. Isaac and Obu stood up to join us.

The first lesson in teaching them to live off the land was showing them the food that was available to eat and seed. They were familiar with most of them - avocados, oranges, and pineapple growing in the higher regions. And durian, guava and melons growing in the lowlands.

Most important was teaching them the value of each food and herb to keep their bodies strong and healthy. There was a remedy for everything growing out of the ground. Isaac, Ishmael, and Obu already felt at home. They each carried armfuls of fruit they chopped down themselves back to their shelters.

When the evening rolled around and we started a bonfire, I began the ritual that would come to be our nightly routine. I handed Isaac a piece of parchment that I wrote the night's lecture on for him to recite. He cleared his throat and hushed everyone's chatter for them to listen to my words.

"Abraham has written us our first lecture. Everyone quiet down and listen." Then he began, "*How a Human Learns*

From a Bird, by Abraham of Paradise…if you want to learn from Birds of Paradise, you must become humans of paradise. Pay close attention to every little detail of the land; the sound of growth, the smell of rebirth, the feel of splendor. Grant the forest your senses and it will acquaint you with a whole new system to live by."

Isaac then read an instruction I wrote on the page to blow out the bonfire and recite the last line.

"Then we won't be able to see…" he whispered at me, confused.

I nodded at him and he grabbed a jug of water. Pouring it over the fire, darkness descended on the gathering. The moonlight and starlight shed highlights against the pure darkness of every human face. "Now all your faces are the same color. Every bird's feathers appear just as plain. We are one as if we closed our eyes. Thank you."

The group gave my lecture a standing ovation.

That night, I returned to the cabin to work on my novel and write the next night's lecture. With all the food consumed and the seeds gathered, I felt as though it might be time to teach these humans how to garden.

Just as I expected, they took to it naturally because their talent to garden was ingrained in their source code. It was much closer to human nature to love and nurture than harm each other or the Earth. Their tendencies to be cruel were external to their humanity. They were acting anything but human when they exploited each other.

34

Gardening Tip Number One
Tending the Soil

Human civilization has always lent itself to be symbolized by a garden. How humans tend to it will determine whether that garden produces bountiful splendor or social rot. The taste of a garden's fruit is dictated by the health and ingredients of its soil. A civilization's soil is its ideas.

The modern world didn't go wrong because of a snowballing of bad, callous choices. It was the ideas underpinning modernity itself that caused the system to fail from the very beginning.

The only way this new civilization can flourish is by laying the purest soil. Love and compassion over materialism. Acceptance of death as a part of life. An ingrained ability to let go. Equality among beings, non-violence, and ego-death as the gateway into adulthood.

The modern world wasn't purely evil, and the ancient world wasn't purely good. The modern world used faithfulness in God and relationships as a soil ingredient. This made for a more beautiful garden than soil made with ancient ingredients like collectivism. To that point, freedom is a necessary ingredient in any successful garden. However, to ensure success and health last, soil composed of freedom in proportionate parts to obedience is suggested.

Free beings under God grow godly fresh gardens, but even they need to make some changes. When your fruits sour and your leaves dry out all too soon, tend to the soil before you trim the leaves. Even worse than the bad ideas that built the modern world was humanity's inability to change and replace them with good ones. This is the first principal of nature that must be instilled in the new gardeners of Eden: Change. Gardens that don't change according to their needs perish. Listen to the needs of your people. Plants ready to die are hard and stuck in place. Plants filled with life are soft and flexible.

Part Three
Nature as Media

35

Love in Paradise

Two couples fell in love right under our beaks. The birds would never admit it, but we observed every detail of their romances as closely as possible. Every bird would stay up and fill every branch of every tree, not daring to make a noise, in the hopes of watching the couples.

Delilah and Isaac were the first couple to fall totally in love with each other. Every day they would walk through the forest holding hands and absorbing the beauty of paradise together. Humans, who were conditioned to require constant stimulation, forgot how to appreciate nature. It took them some time to remember this essential skill.

Meanwhile, Delilah and Isaac retaught themselves how to look at nature and experience it differently every time, much the same way the animals do. They would walk the same paths and notice different flowers or leaves, *really notice them*. When nature learned they fancied each other, it grew and changed in ways that enhanced their love.

After a while, Karen began to look at Ishmael with eyes full of the kind of admiration that birds began to unmistakably recognize as human love. Ishmael's eyes would tear up any time he thought of loving again, let alone loving Karen.

Whenever they held hands, the soil beneath their feet could sense them walking together and suddenly, bees were summoned to pollinate the flowers around them. Fruits would fall off their branches; perfectly ripe to eat.

Nature made every accommodation for its gardeners to fall in love because nature had just as much to gain out of their fruitfulness.

The first time Ishmael and Karen kissed; Ishmael was a bit hesitant. He did not want to taint the memory of his wife and twin daughters lost in the great catastrophe. Karen stepped in first, planting the kiss like it was a seed of love in between the folds of Ishmael's brain.

Ishmael's past didn't fade away so much as it was recycled into new, fertile soil to plant a new life. I would watch all this romance around me and think I was some kind of love guru, writing down a lecture about love for the night's bonfire.

I asked Captain Obu to read it, seeing as my two boys were in love and it would be best if they were listening instead of orating. Obu stood up in front of the gang, holding the parchment I had given him; then began to speak.

"The very first thing God asks of humanity is to be fruitful and multiply. He doesn't ask you to love, but *you* made love conditional to that fruitfulness. Birds had no idea what true love was until you came around. It is best for humans not to be like birds. It is better for birds to love like humans. There are plenty of females for a bird or human male to fall in love with, but there is also only one soulmate for every bird or human. Just like there is a day for night, a moon for sun, there is a man for a woman. When birds finally learned how to love and we decided to change our ways completely, all of nature changed with us, adapting to reflect the beauty it saw in us. In this way, you have been gardening paradise simply by existing pure of heart."

36

Gardening Tip Number Two
Trimming Leaves

If a civilization's soil is its ideas, then the plants must be its people. Bad soil grows corrupted life and in time, the garden can become so full of foulness it will come to recognize the ugly growth as beautiful.

Again, this was the case for the modern world. The spirit of competition was a fundamental part of the soil. Global capitalism inspired some of the most advanced technology imaginable. However, the fruits of that economic system often overshadowed the rot and depravity in some of its creations.

Such suffering was brought about by the need for the rich to starve others so they could feed themselves fancily. Though the garden grew high and mighty, it still fell under its own weight. It was man's greatest folly to create a society that desires to be paradise but is built upon principals that conflict with what they know paradise is.

Once you've grown a garden on bad ideas, you'll be stuck with some healthy leaves and some ugly, dying ones. So, what's the best way to identify which to trim?

There are those that give everything to others. Then

there are those that give everything of themselves to themselves and tell you others benefit from it. If they have no time for charity, if they deceive without regret, and if they cannot love another, they ought to be trimmed off the tree - but that doesn't mean getting rid of them.

By trimming, I mean rebuking them. The way Jesus carried His tongue like a sword, you too must wield a tongue sharp enough to speak truth to power. For nothing else can dismantle power. Nothing will topple a garden quicker than power accumulating at the top or a lack of truth at the root.

This is no inditement of the rich and powerful. You can be poor and meek, but no good for a garden. For instance, many people find transgression beautiful. Some poets and artists find more inspiration from rotten vegetables than ripe fruit.

When a garden is so beautiful and shinning that the plants take on uniform appearances, then perhaps ugliness has its place to make the whole more unique.

However, if the society gets overwhelmed by ugliness, it's the transgressive art that vanishes first. Artists that made art about ugly things found patrons when the world was beautiful but when the world fell to catastrophe, no one wanted to hear a peep out of them. When the world is in pain in something so vicious and sweeping as a war, toxic event, or epidemic, the art that people want affirms the human spirit.

37

Nature is a Language Can You Read?

After much time tending to nature, nature began tending to humans. Their bodies began adapting to the heat, the cold, the rain, and all the poisons of the forest. They each plugged into the system, so now their eyes could read the land to know where the seeds ought to be planted and where the water ought to be poured.

Nature writes and speaks just as much as nature itself is the language. So, when the humans immersed themselves in their gardening, their minds were groomed to recognize the characters and intonations nature used to speak. The way a branch splinters or a vine curls can be how a plant communicates its soul.

The gardeners began to see these signs and interpret them to give each plant the care it asked for. Some trees were trimmed shorter, some were watered more, others were uprooted and moved into the sun, some into the shade.

The more they all worked together, the more the garden started taking shape, as if once nature had human arms and legs, it started making more sense, taking on a geometry it always intended for itself. Though it could never be truly finished, the garden started to feel like paradise.

New fruits began to grow and never before seen animals began to inhabit the garden. When I gave Isaac a note asking him where these animals came from, he told me, "The garden invited them here."

I could see now the humans became closer to nature than the birds. I should have expected this considering if the gardeners aren't aware of what was happening in their garden, then no one is. I could see a change in their consciousness simply by looking into their eyes where the civilized fog they used to carry had cleared up. Clarity was beaten into their minds simply by bracing the elements until they regained their senses.

Being one with nature is a lost sense worth regaining. Actually, it's a group of senses; a form of omniscience, really. If humans knew what they were missing, living in the cities, playing video games, speaking over cell phones, driving cars, flying in planes, they would yearn to return to nature's oneness.

Television doesn't so much wash a brain as it does wipe it clean. It kept humans in one place, indoors, staring at images that sapped their imaginations - images they were convinced were somehow useful. The ones that watched too much television were the most susceptible to the great catastrophe, the ones that used nature for the same function had a much better chance to survive.

<h1 style="text-align:center">38</h1>

Gardening Tip Number Three
Picking Fruit

Gardens exist for people to pick their produce. The produce of a civilization are its innovations and art. If you examine the world before it fell apart, every one of their creations were screaming the end was near.

Writers were so obsessed with the end of the world, their stories cascaded into a horror show of every event they predicted. If you asked these writers how they felt once they saw their lives being destroyed by the very calamities they subconsciously wished for, none of them were proud of their clairvoyance. They came to regret what they created. They wished they had created something beautiful because, in their darkest hour, the only creations they could cling to were just as ugly as the reality that would slowly eat their lives up whole.

The same was true of technology. There came a point the creators of every new invention knew exactly how detrimental it would be to humanity.

These included every new surveillance accessory, the new application to force digital dependency, and the new intelligence to replace human stupidity, laziness, ego, and imperfection. A machine has no chance of ever tapping into nature and even less of a chance to overpower it.

When a man perishes, they become part of the Earth. When a machine perishes, Earth buries it. Machines are forgotten. Humans become a part of the Earth's living memory.

The point of all this is to pick the fruit that's pure of soul - the art and innovation you can depend on to feed the people.

39

How Humans Taught the Birds

Ever since the birds began mingling with humans, they started picking up their behaviors. A male bird would now watch a female just as long as a female would watch a male.

The male would take longer to choose who to love, basing their decision on a wide variety of factors. Courtship was no longer about winning whoever was willing. A kind heart took a bird a long way.

Females still steered the direction of the species, ultimately choosing who would be blessed with a love to fall into. Ever since this happened, courtship displays became more personalized toward the female.

Displays weren't about trying to look or sound pleasing to everyone. After generations adapted to this change in behavior, chicks would be born with certain colors or feathers that would personalize them to certain females.

When the human world began falling apart, females and males changed their courting rituals because with resources so low, they couldn't just go around flirting with anyone all the time anymore.

Birds, too, learned about humility and sacrifice. Now, when a female gave birth to a chick, the male would stay and watch them grow. The birds would live out their Shade Songs, giving the verses new meaning.

We did not mourn for the old way of life, in fact, we forgot it rather quickly. You could see on the faces of the male birds how love had imbued their very being.

With families to raise and no interest in new females to court, you might assume the father Birds of Paradise would stop dancing.

This proved to be wrong because if a female ever felt her male was no longer in love with her and didn't care to dance for her anymore then the female would just leave, taking her chicks with her. Such was the case for a certain King of Saxony.

King Bob lost his wife and two chicks after years of bitterness that culminated in a sour dance display that saw him fall flat on his face. He became the laughingstock of paradise's royal class. Dejected by his family and community, the King saw no other option than to jump off the tallest branch in the forest and free fall - resulting in a broken wing.

After hearing his pleas for help, the lowland birds were so alarmed by the sight of seeing him hurt after his big fall, they spread the news throughout the entire island. If a bird could hurt itself in paradise, then paradise must have lost a vital piece of its harmony.

When the birds looked for a scapegoat, they knew it was a result of their interaction with humans, but none of them were audacious enough to speak up and dispute the Mother Bird's vision.

Every bird but me I should say, because my fury was immediate and directly targeted at my own humans. I summoned Isaac to my cabin one morning while the other humans planted new trees.

He opened the door to see me standing by a piece of paper. He walked over and sat down; then took one of two pencils so the two of us could have a conversation.

"Maybe this was a big mistake," I accidentally chirped

aloud before writing.

"Why do you say that?" Isaac answered.

For a second, I thought I could speak English, but then I realized it was the humans that learned how to understand birds. I put my pencil down and kept talking.

"The more human the birds become, the more problems we acquire. We don't want human problems."

"Then stay birds."

"It's too late. The birds like having names, families."

"But they don't want pain?"

"How did you know about King Bob?"

"The humans have learned from the birds too, Abraham. We heard what you all were singing."

"How do you suggest we stop the birds from experiencing human pain?"

"Birdly nature has taught us how to cope with it ourselves. Perhaps the birds became so mesmerized by the ways of humans they forgot the ways of birds."

I left our meeting with the goal of calling all the birds to audience so I may address King Bob's fall. That night, we left the humans without a lecture. I gathered all the Birds of Paradise at the broken statue of the Mother Bird.

"Birds of Paradise, we have to talk about Bob."

With his wing in a sling, King Bob jumped off his branch to speak directly to my face, "It's your fault we birds have become so self-centered as to think jumping off branches could help us stop the pain of losing someone you love - you're the one who asked these humans to change us without a care for how."

Before I could even refute his statement, a wind blew that every bird knew was the Mother Bird returning from the spirit world. From the dust in the wind, her body was sculpted and with the breath of God. She was animated to step in between myself and this King of Saxony.

"You listen here," she confronted King Bob, "You have

no right to blame the actions of a bird on any other bird or human. Now that we all know the emotional pains that come with love, the very pains King Bob succumbed to, we still consider true love worth pursuing, don't we?"

Every bird unanimously agreed with their Mother.

"We have no choice but to accept it. Just like death is a part of life, so is hurt a part of love. Love is not easy. Love makes you confront all your fears and insecurities. If you're not willing to do that, don't even try."

40

Gardening Tip Number Four
Sowing Seed

What determines how quickly and powerfully a seed germinates is the thoughtfulness with which it was sown. A seed needs enough space apart from the rest and enough water to feed until its ready to sprout shoots.

Like children, the seeds grow into giant and beautiful plants, producing whatever their God-given purpose it was to produce. They all look the same at this stage of their lives, yet there is no way to know exactly what will become of them.

By the time the modern world came closest to its end, the garden had grown so ugly and unhealthy, people preferred their children just stay indoors to grow apart from the world altogether.

Then, when those children became adults, none were equipped with the proper skills to do anything but lay down and quit when the world finally ended.

For the majority of human history, adults knew their children had to face pain and adversity from an early age if they ever wanted to thrive.

You see, the seeds of house plants have harder times growing in the chaos of the forest. The humans of this garden know they must raise their children as warriors and not just gardeners because someday, someone will have to defend this garden.

41

The First and Second Wedding

It was a very hot day in the garden when the men looked up and realized all the women stayed behind at camp. They figured not to ask why and just put in double the day's load; picking up a sweat under the brutal sun to make sure every bit of produce was harvested and every seed was sown to keep the harvest cycle unshaken.

When the day was finally done and the men returned home, they decided not to resent their women for leaving all the work to them.

Instead, the men acted like nothing happened, suspecting the women would be dying to tell them why they were missing. Isaac laid down in his bed and watched from out the cracks in the walls of his shelter at all the women leaving Delilah's side now that her soul-mate returned.

Delilah scurried over to join Isaac in bed, seemingly as tired as Isaac. They laid there together and Isaac just silently stared off into space; as if paying space more attention would surely be a proper annoyance.

"Did you have a nice day?" Delilah asked.

Isaac shrugged with as little care as possible, taking a dragging moment to speak. "Sure," he wavered.

A long, deep sigh from out Isaac's tired ribs sunk him

deeper into his bed, too low for Delilah to look him in the eye.

"Was anything different about today?"

"Not really. Same as ever."

Isaac turned away from her for Delilah to watch his side rise and fall in an insulting, feigned sleep. She slapped him hard across the ribs as if knowing exactly which muscles ached the most. Isaac seethed; then turned to Delilah. "What?"

"Aren't you going to ask me where I was? Where all the girls were?"

"I didn't even notice you were gone..." he started laughing before he could finish his sentence.

"Shut up. You're not funny."

"Tell me. Where were you all day?"

"Guess."

Isaac rolled his eyes and tossed his head around to think. "...uh, you were cooking us a surprise dinner?"

"Nope. Guess again."

"Are you pregnant?"

She was shocked he guessed correctly, slapping him again for stealing the joy she would get from telling him herself.

"How did you know?" she shouted.

"Because I love you, babe. I can tell."

"Are you happy?"

Isaac sat up to look into Delilah's eyes as a layer of gloss rolled over them. "This is what we always wanted. Our baby is the first born here. They will be a very special child and we will teach them to be a strong, beautiful soul. I love you, Delilah. You're going to be an incredible mom."

I watched them embrace, kiss, and cry together from my cabin. In these matters, there was no wisdom I could impart to the humans. I watched, wanting to learn everything about the process of how a couple raise their child.

From here on, the men were relegated to the garden

while the women stayed at camp to help Delilah as she started to show. Her belly began growing bigger than her body knew how to adapt for. The female birds all noticed and came to Delilah's aid. They flew her all the berries, nuts, and herbs they could from every part of the forest. They sang to her and the child in her belly.

That night before the evening's bonfire, Isaac approached me to ask, "Abraham. Can I read my own lecture tonight?"

"What does it say?"

"It's a proposal to Delilah."

"A proposal for what?"

"Marriage."

"Ah, of course, you have my blessing," I told Isaac.

With the fire crackling in the center of our gathering, every man, woman, and bird in attendance was shocked when Isaac bent down to one knee and spoke directly from his heart to a happy, sobbing Delilah.

"Sweetheart, I never knew the beauty of life until I met you. Every horrible thing we survived was meant to bring us together on this beautiful island. I'd choose to live this life a hundred times over just to fall in love with you every time. I love you forever and need to know, will you marry me?"

"Yes."

Isaac shot up off his knee and lifted Delilah off the ground to kiss her. Everyone clapped and the birds pecked their branches to make a joyous ruckus that filled the night. Every day after that, the skies were filled with the streaks of flying females, scrambling through the forest to get Delilah everything she could need for the most paradise wedding.

To make her dress, every male offered their plumes, feathers, ribbons, and wires. The dress was so radiant, no pair of eyes could completely take-in the sight of it without some kind of tear-jerking or heartbreaking awe.

It featured the blue feathers of a Superb, the wires off a

Twelve Wired Bird's behind, the Carola's white plumage, the King's reds, the Wilson's yellows, the King of Saxony's ribbon's, and the Emperor's fluffy flanks. It was a dress that served a rainbow's function, like a promise from God to keep the new world safe.

Before the wedding, Delilah asked me to walk her down the aisle and Isaac asked Sarah to do the same for him. The humans considered us birds their "spirit parents." Perhaps far into the future, the next myths of humanity's origins would claim humans were the offspring of birds.

The day of Isaac and Delilah's wedding, the aisle running down to the alter was lined with every flower on the island.

The congregation stood in place as Isaac walked down the aisle with Sarah in tow and Sarah joined the birds to leave Isaac at the alter to await his Delilah.

I walked Delilah down the aisle as a few fluttering birds held the tails of her dress in their beaks, giving her the ethereal and ghostly feel of floating.

Isaac didn't cry when he first saw his wife to be. He stood up straight and strong, an example to every bird as to what it meant to be a man.

As they stood there together in silence, simply taking each other in, Captain Obu began to speak.

"We are here to celebrate the love between Isaac Kesher and Delilah Abebe."

When it came time for each one to recite their vows, Isaac went first.

"Never did I think this Jewish kid from Tel Aviv would marry a black girl from Ethiopia, but God brought us together for a purpose. We are here to protect this forest just as we are here to protect each other. The more I love you, the more the world prospers with us, because of us."

After Delilah delivered her vows, Captain Obu led Isaac through the central vow that determined the rest of their lives, "I, Isaac Kesher, take you Delilah Abebe to be my lawfully wedded wife to have and to hold, from this day forward, for better, for worse, for richer, for poorer, in sickness and in health, until death do us part."

Delilah concurred and the two kissed and were pronounced husband and wife. As the happy couple frolicked down the aisle together under a whirlwind of petals, Karen and Ishmael wondered how their ceremony would differ.

Ishmael didn't wait to get Karen pregnant, he got down on one knee and asked her to be his wife once Isaac and Delilah were gone.

Paradise rejoiced, enchanted by the glory of human love. During the party that followed, Delilah threw the bouquet and once the flowers went flying, all the female birds shot after them.

Sarah made sure she was the first to snag them in her beak and fly them to safety where she could cry tears of joy that she would finally be married.

It was only a week later that Ishmael and Karen were married and, after their wedding, Ishmael and Isaac came to me in my cabin to personally thank me.

"You are named after the father of religion, the father of Ishmael and Isaac," said Isaac.

"A little bird for a father," Ishmael said. "It makes sense to me. You've always looked after us. We owe you our lives and our wives."

"We just wanted to say thank you, Abraham. For everything," said Isaac.

"Yes, Abraham. Thank you. We are eternally grateful," Ishmael agreed.

"You're both very welcome."

"We brought you a gift," said Ishmael.

Isaac pulled his hand out from behind his back to reveal a tiny box. He laid the box down upon the table and took off the top. Inside was the tiniest tuxedo made for a bird.

I put it on and suddenly felt rather dapper, sashaying down the table, strutting my stuff.

"This must be what a man feels like; strong and stiff, every step with so much conviction."

"You look good, but you'd look better with a girl on your arm."

"He's right. When do you think you're going to pop the question to Sarah?"

"I have to finish my book first. It's the only thing I can think about."

"Hopefully she'll wait for you."

"Of course, she will. Sarah and I love each other. Now, if you don't mind, I'd like to get back to work. Thank you both for this present, my sons, I will put it to good use. You'll see." I winked.

The boys left me to my solitude and in the cabin's solace. I felt loneliness and longing. I wondered if this was what Sarah was feeling now without me. I'm sure I owe her an apology for my absence but for now all I can do is use this longing to inspire some beautiful words. It's going to be a long night for me. I'm going to finish my book.

42

Gardening Tip Number Five
Watering the Plants

I've come up with all these metaphors for you. The garden is civilization. The seeds are our children. The plants are you people. The fruits are your art. The soil, your ideas.

What is the water though? What feeds and nourishes you to live and be good people? It's that spice of life, the little things people do to make a boring day feel special so they don't fall victim to all life's troubles.

It's that sort of magic a person has to wield to uplift a simple moment into something worth remembering.

When man's ordinary magic has been exhausted out of them, then evil has finally won.

What feeds humans the way water feeds plants? It's their humanity. It's already a part of them.

Humans can never forget their own humanity.

43

The End of My Story

Finishing my book was my sole priority the moment I returned to paradise from my journey. The humans and the birds rarely saw me. I was only present around the bonfire to lead lecture. During the days and late into the nights, I stayed indoors, working to the bone.

I was more deeply imprisoned by the will to write than during my actual kidnapping. That kidnapping taught me the importance of patience and, in a weird way, was the greatest blessing ever bestowed on me.

My book spanned my whole life's story from being a chick raised by my beautiful mother to my feathers changing color to meeting Sarah.

The story didn't end there though, it included my journey across the oceans and even prophesized my future, marrying Sarah in a beautiful wedding and giving birth to chicks that would make us so happy.

I didn't want to be brash, thinking I could write Sarah's destiny for her and condense it to a string of words I could dream up at will.

I knew the reality of our love would prove to be very different from what I imagined. Our love could only be determined by Sarah and how she followed her heart.

163

Once Abraham and Sarah exchanged vows in the book, there was nothing left to write. There was much more I could imagine after our wedding - chicks to raise, nests to build, even my own end.

There was a certain sacrifice I made to lead the humans to paradise. I paid for their entry with a few years of my life. I figured those years I would've used to take care of Sarah, making sure above all things that as we got old enough for the years to start taking our life little by little, I would do everything in my power to uphold her dignity in her old age. And if I don't live long enough to care for her, our chicks will do it for me.

Once the book was finished, I felt a huge weight lift off my wings. Words and thoughts in a writer's mind can often feel like anchors until they're expelled onto paper.

This must be the closest a man can come to know the feeling of giving birth to a child, this cluster of thought inside some spiritual cavity in me was removed to live a life of its own.

If I was lucky, my art would take flight out the nest and not fall to its death. I was lighter now, flying more freely, my thoughts too lucid to walk straight or steady.

Mentally, I was swimming through a lush stream of consciousness, not thinking at all, simply feeling and absorbing the world around me, enjoying the blurring facets of its texture.

When I stepped out of the cabin, the light nearly blinded me. Every being that saw me return to the world could tell I finished my book. I was rather disheveled, unable to bear reality after spending so much time in my imagination.

I wanted to see Sarah to apologize for my absence, but I would soon learn it wouldn't be easy. I realized that with all the time I spent finishing my book, I had paid her no attention whatsoever. She sacrificed so much for me already and I made her endure more neglect waiting for me while I was only a stone's throw away.

When I found her resting on her favorite branch and landed beside her, she quickly flew away before I could apologize. This happened everywhere I found her. Whenever she saw me, she would split. I'd have to trap her to get a word in, hoping we could be each other's hostages, holding our loves ransom.

I learned human love was no breeze. The human heart is about the size of a fist, a Bird of Paradise's heart is the size of a nut. Perhaps human love is just too big for a bird's heart to handle. There was no hope for Sarah to be mine forever if I couldn't commit to put my ambitions behind our love. I'd rather be her soulmate than a writer. There were few writers in this world but believe me, there are fewer soulmates actually wise enough to marry.

I went out on a limb and flew across the island to the statue of the Mother Bird. That's where I found Sarah, sitting there with the statue and the dead flowers from Delilah's bouquet. She would come here to commune with the spirits.

She'd close her eyes and see it all play in her mind like a dream that lasted for as long as she wanted to watch. She could see what happened before and after the Birds of Paradise.

These dreams told her our future before I ever acted upon any destinies. This was her journey, a clairvoyant bird, with gifted vision after she sang the Shade Song.

She saw everything. That's why she waited for me. She knew I would return. She saw my book's finish and my arrival here. When I landed at her side and slowly walked up, she opened her eyes out of her trance and decided to stay.

"If you're going to apologize, save it. It'll only make me more hurt."

"I'm such an idiot," I said.

"I know."

"Sarah, I had to finish."

"You didn't have to act like I didn't exist. I know where I fit in your priorities now."

"All I wrote about was you though. There is page after page about only you."

"Really?"

"Yes."

"What did you say?"

"I wrote about how much I love you, about how much our love means to me. I even imagined our wedding."

"Our wedding?"

"Yes."

"Are you proposing to me?"

I realized exactly the predicament I talked myself into. She guided me to this place but, knowing this was the destination of every path I'd ever dare tread, I didn't feel one bit tricked.

"I believe we need a witness," I said with a wiggle in my throat, trying to backstep.

Not letting me pull out of love's clutches, a great wind swelled up at our feet and from out the dust there she was, the Mother Bird.

"I've been watching all along but, if I need to be present, here I am," she affirmed.

Bouncing my eyes between the Mother Bird and Sarah, I didn't bother fighting it anymore. I got down to one knee and asked for her wing in marriage.

"Sarah, you are the most beautiful bird in the world. I could never have imagined I would be lucky enough to love you. For as long as I live, I will write about our love and live those words every day. Sarah of Paradise, will you marry me?"

"No."

"No?" I asked.

"You don't deserve me. Not now."

"After everything!?"

"Look at you, so full of expectations. I am not beholden to you. We are only beholden to our words and you haven't loved me half as much as you say you do."

"I know. But we have our whole lives ahead of us."

"Enough time to find another bird to love?"

"I don't want to love another bird. I only want to love you," I started to sob.

"Why me?"

"You were the only one that ever believed in me. I couldn't even believe in myself without you. If you don't love me, I'll be a wreck."

"Do you want to love me? Or do you want to marry me?"

"I want to marry you so I can love you forever as my wife."

As she looked into my eyes, her gaze began to break as she started crying too. "After all the tears you made me shed, I just wanted you to cry me a river. Now that you put it that way, I believe you. Let's get married."

My eyes opened wide as I realized she accepted the life I dreamed up for us. I stood up off my knee and held her. The Mother Bird smiled for all of paradise was pleased.

44

Gardening Tip Number Six
On the Tree of Knowledge
Of God and Evil

Adam and Eve were expelled from paradise for eating the forbidden fruit on the tree of Knowledge of Good and Evil.

Those that wrote the Bible did the same as me, transforming elements of the human condition into nature metaphors. The act of eating the fruit was not evil itself. It was simply a necessary step in destiny's looping routine. For as long as humans and nature exist on the Earthly realm, the first law of the Earth is change. Paradise changes. Humans will leave. They will desire something more; harmony and order is not enough.

Humans will go back out into the world once every robot is rusted to the core and every oppressor long dead. Humans will reclaim the world and make it good again. The world will be good until it once again becomes evil and it will then be evil until it returns to goodness.

The Tree of Knowledge simply triggers the first step. Humans will grow so desirous of change they will disobey their own God for a fresh start.

When the Tree of Knowledge of Good and Evil finally sprouts in our garden, I will instruct the humans to let it grow. When the forbidden fruit finally ripens, I will let them eat it and bid them farewell.

At that moment of first bite, the humans will taste the beginning of their own destiny and nothing tastes better than knowing you have a destiny, trust me, I know.

45

The First Bird Wedding

If there was ever a moment birds wished they were humans, it would have to be this; with Sarah in the purest white gown and I in my black tuxedo. What humans and birds shared was the knowledge that feminine grace came in the form of a pure, solid, plain color. My groomsmen were Isaac and Ishmael. Sarah's bridesmaids were Delilah and Karen.

When I walked down the aisle and reached the alter, I suddenly felt the most burning anxiety in my stomach. It was a fear so sudden and paralyzing I nearly crumpled under its gravity. Isaac pet my head and I looked up at him.

"Don't sweat it, man. Everything is going to be golden."

"Right," I nodded.

As the music began to play, Sarah appeared at the end of the aisle and waddled down to me under paradise's impeccable setting sun.

When her eyes arrived level to mine, we were lost in the absolute loveliness of each other at our life's most important moment. I could've spilled every beautiful word I had to say to her right there, gushing over how I'd give her my very soul, but I held back.

The secret to human and birdly love is the same;

holding back but keeping true. The procession began and the Mother Bird spoke.

"We are gathered here today to celebrate the love between Abraham and Sarah. A love humanity owes everything to."

Truer words were never spoken, for as inspired as we were by humans, all would be dead if it wasn't for her love for me.

As the Mother Bird spoke, I began to zone out, the anxiety in my stomach boiled over and began to speak. I couldn't hear the Mother Bird over this internal voice that started stirring.

"Abraham," the voice began.

"Yes?"

"Once you marry this bird, I have another journey for you."

"Who are you?"

"I Am what I Am."

"I see. I am not worthy. What is it you want me to do?"

"Be fruitful and multiply all over this Earth. Where you go, paradise follows. You must seed paradise all over this Earth."

"You want us to leave the island?"

"Yes. You are not needed here anymore. The garden will grow larger and healthier than you can imagine. The birds will learn to love each other and themselves. You and Sarah will have many beautiful children."

"I accept this journey."

"Good. I will come with you and, when your wings weigh heavy, I will carry you through the sky."

When I returned back to my own body, the entire congregation was staring at me, perturbed. Sarah and the Mother Bird's faces were red with burning rage.

"One more time…Do you Abraham of Paradise, take Sarah of Paradise to be your lawfully wedded wife to have and to hold, from this day forward, for better, for worse, for richer, for poorer, in sickness and in health, until death do you part?"

"I do."

As quickly as a blink, the anger left Sarah's face and she smiled at me with a joy that was uniquely eternal. It's the joy that resides in a sacred pocket of a woman's heart for as long as she and her husband live as one. I would see that joy more often throughout my life than most husbands do.

I was very good to Sarah in our time and gave her many chicks. We would share laughs and tears of joy on many, many occasions.

Needless to say, she accepted me as her husband. It was the greatest moment of my life and whenever I'm down, I remember her eyes on that day. I remember our sunset.

Our love is a heaven on Earth that could cull fire and turn brimstone into forest.

Do Birds of Paradise believe in heaven? Yes, of course I do. I believe in Sarah and I above all other things.

46

Gardening Tip Number Seven
Restoring a Broken Vase

Ancient Judaic texts compare the world to a broken vase. The role of a gardener is to collect all the shards to make the vase whole again. One can use vines to pull every shard into place and a bird's spittle to glue them together.

In a broken world, humans harm others and themselves. They are not born to harm a fly or branch though.

Repairing the world will repair the human. So please, aid each other in gathering these pieces and together, wholeness will be achieved by you all.

Then the vase is ready for roses.

47

Epilogue

Sarah never heard the voice that told me to be fruitful, multiply, and leave paradise. She believed I did though and we left the home of our parents and grandparents to start a new life on lands we never knew.

By this time, the Earth had changed again. The metals made by humans were swallowed up by unrestricted nature. Lands once civilized became gardens run amuck. The machines were rusted to the core, vines growing in and out of them, with no hope to ever escape.

The men that made these machines who fled underground were stuck there until the world above forgot all about their terrible designs for the future of Earth and humanity. There were no more oppressors.

On this land, there were only the plants and animals. Still, we bred and lived like we were in hiding; in attics or industrial ribbing. We gave birth to chicks we would raise to maturity then leave on the land to spread paradise. We did this like clockwork on continent after continent.

Still, there were no people, publishers, or bookstores for my book. Every bird I ever raised, learned English by reading my book. Those birds told others my story until suddenly, the kinship of animals became connected by my fable.

The story of how nature chose humans to garden was a love letter to humanity from nature. Even though humanity was an imperfect lover, nature can be spiteful too. Still, nature never forgot humanity's tenderness.

Years later, after we were long dead, Sarah and I became one with the wind just like the Mother Bird. We had one foot in the spirit world and the other in the material one because we always considered ourselves guardians of Earth.

We would watch everything and, for as long as I watched, every part of the world grew more and more like paradise.

Watching my birds grow up and have chicks of their own was a beautiful way to pass eternity.

We could've gone on this way for many more decades, but something was missing. There was a big hole in my heart no bird could fill. What I wanted to see was destiny. Sarah assured me it would come.

It took a while, but when destiny finally arrived on the shores of all the continents, it came bearing plenty of humans to set foot upon the land. I could see Isaac's eyes or Delilah's smile in some of them.

These humans came to build, using the trees grown out of the fallout from the last catastrophe. They built houses and mills. They built wells and pools. They built all these things, but didn't build any fences.

No one thought to fear a neighbor. These were truly my children just as much as my chicks. Humans in harmony, nature in harmony, humans as a part of nature, it all came full circle.

Eventually, one human decided it was a good idea to print words upon parchment. They had many oral myths they could print; oral myths men created over bonfires.

But there was one story that had to be published first.

"The Story of Abraham" was printed in the thousands and copies were spread far and wide.

Not a single book was sold, but every reader cherished every word. My words became an essential guide to connecting with the essence of being. Those that read it would live calmer lives with cooler heads and love more fondly.

No matter how much this group of humans tried not to destroy nature, a few evil men couldn't help but disrupt the peace. Those evil men seduced more men to think chaos could make for a better garden.

I could see it coming. Maybe in a few hundred years, another ugly age would come to pay tribute to the dystopias of futures past. Who knows what form the next catastrophe will take?

Regardless, all will suffer and all will mend. It makes me very happy to see that no matter what, the world will keep on spinning. The evil of men no longer upsets me.

There's no amount of human brutality that the world can't handle. Everything is going to be alright.

END

About the Author

Robert Shepyer is a published novelist, produced screenwriter, filmmaker, and music blogger. Growing up as a Jewish rocker and 'cinephile' in Los Angeles inspired every bit of his prose and world view.

www.ingramcontent.com/pod-product-compliance
Lightning Source LLC
Chambersburg PA
CBHW021333190726
48288CB00003B/1096